THE VETERAN

A. RIVERS

To my husband.
For listening to me rant about how
the characters in my head weren't
doing what I told them to.

PROLOGUE

Two suitcases sat on the front porch as I walked up the stairs after school had let out for the day. They were my father's, but I couldn't remember him mentioning that he was going anywhere. Frowning, I entered the hallway, intending to find him and ask what was happening, but raised voices coming from the living room stopped me.

I winced. They were fighting again. It seemed like Mom and Dad were always arguing these days. Sometimes, I wished they'd just get a divorce so I didn't have to listen to them yell at each other anymore. At least I'd be out of here in a few months. I'd been accepted into a prestigious dramatic arts college and would be moving into a dorm until I finished my studies.

Deciding I'd rather not face my parents while they were angry, I turned off the hallway and into my bedroom. Their voices grew louder so I closed the door to drown them out. Back when they'd first started fighting, I'd tried to figure out what their disagreements were about so I could help, but that hadn't done anything other than upset them more than they already were. I'd learned it was best to give them space when they were like this.

I stripped off my school uniform and changed into a pair of patterned jeans and a t-shirt advertising my friend's band, then paused for a moment, listening hard. When I realized they were still going at it, I grabbed a bright pink nail polish from the cabinet and sat on the floor to paint my toenails. I'd finished one foot and started the other when an almighty crash echoed through the house.

My hand slipped, smearing nail polish across my toe. My heart thumped madly as I waited for the arguing to resume, but there was only silence. Eerie silence. After so many months of being a bystander for these fights, I knew what was normal and what wasn't. Something was wrong.

My pulse beating a rapid tattoo, I put the nail polish away and crept down the hall. When I reached the living room door, I edged it open and peered through the gap. Mom was lying on the floor, her long hair splayed around her. She wasn't moving. Dad knelt over her, muttering frantically. He grabbed her shoulders and shook her but she didn't respond. I threw the door open and raced to her side.

"What happened?" I demanded, staring down at her. Her eyes were closed, her face slack. I cupped her head with my hands and felt something wet and sticky. Heart sinking, I withdrew my hands and saw they were coated with blood. I scrambled backward, away from Dad. He watched me, his complexion pale and his eyes wide.

"I didn't mean to," he whispered, looking horrified. "We need to leave, but she wouldn't come. It was taking too long." He dragged a hand through his hair. "I pushed her, and she... she..."

I glanced from Dad to Mom, noticing for the first time that an electrical cable was tangled around her ankle and that her head was only a few inches from the tiles around the fireplace. Red droplets stood out against gray stone. I could imagine exactly what had happened. They'd gotten angry, egging each other on, then he'd shoved her, and she'd tripped and hit her head. And now she wasn't moving.

"I didn't mean to," he repeated, staring blankly. "I'd never—"

"We need to call an ambulance," I snapped, grabbing my phone from my pocket. I started dialing but the sound of a vehicle pulling up the drive made me pause. There weren't any sirens, but perhaps Dad had already called for help. I looked at him to confirm and saw the remaining color leach from his cheeks.

"Go," he hissed, his eyes locking on me. "Out the back, over the fence. Call the police, but whatever you do, don't come back."

I raised my eyebrows. "Are you crazy? Mom needs help. I'm not going anywhere."

He reached behind himself and brandished a gun. I gasped. He leveled it at me, his expression frantic. "Get out, Sage. Right now."

My lips trembled. "You're insane."

He undid the safety. "Go!"

I stumbled away from him, hurrying toward the exit. I yanked the door open and slammed it shut behind me, then sprinted across our short back lawn and around the garden shed, to the broken board in the fence that I could use to climb it. I shoved my foot into the gap and pushed myself up, flinching as what sounded like a gunshot came from the house. I heard a shout, and then men's voices. Terror coursed through me as I fell over the fence and hit the ground on the other side. The rough landing jarred my teeth but I kept my mouth shut and didn't make a noise.

The voices were louder now, and I got to my knees and crept along the edge of the fence, then straightened just enough to see over the timber and into our backyard. My father stood in the center of the lawn, his gun aimed at a man with short brown hair and cruel eyes, who was also armed—as were his two companions. Another man emerged from behind the threesome. He was the shortest of the group, but something in his confident stride told me he was in charge.

"Where is it, Brendan?" the short man demanded as he joined them.

I tasted blood and realized I'd bitten my lip. Should I call out to distract the men, or stay hidden? Dad had sent me away. He must have known they were coming and wanted me gone, but could I really stay here while they were threatening him?

I fumbled for my cell phone and called 911, ducking low so there was no chance of them seeing me.

"I didn't take it," Dad said as I waited for the call to connect. "I swear to you."

A gunshot sounded. Then another. I clutched a hand to my mouth to mask a whimper. Who'd been shot?

"What the fuck?" It was Dad's voice, strained but strong. Thank God. I crawled away from the fence, toward my neighbor's house, and then darted around the side until I was sure the men in my backyard could neither see nor hear me.

"I need the police and an ambulance," I said into the phone, then gave the woman my address. "There are five men with guns. One of them is my dad. My mom is injured." I squeezed my eyes shut. I couldn't bring myself to admit she might be dead.

"Okay, I'll send officers immediately," the woman said. "Are you in a safe place?"

"I think so." Although a few minutes ago, I'd thought home was safe, so who the hell knew for sure?

"Stay put. I'll give the lead officer your phone number and they'll call when it's safe to come out. Do you understand?"

"Yes." We ended the call.

My legs were so shaky I wasn't sure I could move even if I wanted to. I pressed myself against the side of the building, hoping to keep out of sight. I was friendly with the neighbors but if they saw me and said something, they might summon the attention of the men over the fence. I stayed very still, listening intently for any further gunshots, but there were none. Finally, I heard the wail of sirens and slumped in relief. But then, to my horror, someone started shooting.

My heart sunk and tears sprang to my eyes. Somehow, I knew in my bones that once more, everything had gone terribly wrong.

1

8 YEARS LATER

SAGE

The semi-detached town house I now called home was silent as I approached, the front door ajar. I paused, a voice of caution whispering in the back of my mind. After what had happened when I was younger, followed by an incident with my best friend several months ago, I was wary of anything that looked out of place. I knew exactly what nightmares might be lurking out of sight.

I reached into my purse and wrapped my hand around the black tourmaline crystal I kept with me at all times for protection. I slipped it into my left hand and grabbed a can of mace with my right. I might believe in the protective energy of crystals, but I was also practical, and sometimes other means of defense were necessary.

"Jessica!" I called, wondering if my roommate was home and had simply left the door open by mistake. She was a painter and could be forgetful when inspiration struck.

There was no response.

Still, that didn't mean she wasn't here. She might have her headphones on and be listening to music while she worked. But when I stepped into the living room and saw the overturned coffee table, shredded couch cushions, and the hanging painting that had been sliced open, I felt another tingle of wrongness and backtracked out of the house.

On the street, there were enough people around for me to feel safe, so I returned the crystal and mace to my purse and withdrew my cell phone to call the police. After reporting what I'd seen to the dispatcher, I placed another call—to my best friend, Willow.

"Hey, Sage," she said when she answered. "I didn't think you'd be home from yoga class yet."

"Willow." My voice cracked on her name. "Someone has broken into my house."

"Oh, no! Are they still there? Are you okay?" She sounded panicked, and oddly enough, that grounded me. After what Willow and I had been through together when her brother had fallen into debt with some bad people who'd tried to use her to make him pay, I knew she'd understand how shaky I was feeling.

"I think they're gone," I told her. "I saw the damage and left. I'm out by the street. I've already called the police."

"Good," Willow said. "Do you have any idea whether they took anything? It could have been a random robbery."

"I don't know." I pressed my lips together as tears welled in my eyes. "I didn't notice. I got out of there as fast as I could."

"You did the right thing." Willow's tone was soothing and I pressed the phone closer to my ear. I hated the sense that my emotions were slipping out of control. I'd fought hard to manage them over the past few years and I was used to being the calm head in most situations. "I'm coming over," Willow said. "I'll be there as soon as I can."

"Thanks, Will." My lower lip trembled as we said goodbye and hung up. My heartbeat was thundering in my ears and my vision was slightly hazy in that way it got when I was freaking out. I grabbed a hold of a light pole and used it for support. I wouldn't be any good to anyone if I keeled over.

I glanced at the time. Five minutes had passed since I spoke to the dispatcher. The police should be arriving any moment. I scanned the street, relieved to see flashing blue lights in the distance. They drew nearer and screeched to a halt in front of me, double parked. An officer leaped out and another police car appeared behind them.

"Sage Nichols?" the officer asked as she rounded the vehicle that separated her from the sidewalk.

"Yes, that's me." I waved toward the house. "It's that one. I haven't seen anyone come out or go in, but someone has definitely been inside."

"Okay." She nodded briskly and glanced up as another officer joined us. "Is there a rear exit?"

I nodded.

"Levens." She gestured to the male officer. "Go around the back." She turned to me. "Wait here."

I nodded again. With my past, I knew to let the police do their thing. The female officer made her way to the front entrance, drawing her weapon, while her partner went around the exterior of the building. I tensed as they both disappeared out of sight, hoping against hope that I wouldn't hear gunfire. Thankfully, all remained quiet except for the hum of vehicles. A moment later, the female officer exited the building, speaking into her radio. She lowered it as she neared me. Her gaze was shuttered, giving nothing away.

"Do you have a roommate?" she asked.

A trickle of apprehension wormed down my spine. "Yes. Why?"

She ignored my question. "Can you describe her?"

My stomach hardened. "About my height, long brown hair and brown eyes."

Her expression didn't waver, and I got the feeling she'd been expecting that answer.

"What's going on?" I asked. "Is she inside? Is she hurt?"

Why hadn't I checked throughout the house to make sure poor Jessica hadn't been injured? Or had something else happened? Was Jessica responsible for the damage?

"I'm afraid I can't tell you more until my boss arrives," the officer replied.

I felt a pang of certainty that this was more than a simple break-in. Surely they wouldn't need to summon higher ranking officers for anything so trivial. My stomach churned and I was glad I'd missed lunch because at least it meant I was unlikely to throw up.

A dark sedan pulled up alongside us and several people spilled from it. My brows furrowed, then relaxed as Willow's familiar blonde head appeared. She shut the passenger door and raced over, pulling me into a tight embrace. My eyes prickled and threatened to spill over.

"Thank you for coming," I said, my voice thick.

"Of course I came." She rocked me softly before stepping back. "Ronan and Kade are here too. Kade was at our place when you called."

I nodded, too stressed to feel the usual flutters Kade's name would cause. He and Willow's fiancé, Ronan, were two of the three directors of a security company, and I knew they'd help me get to the bottom of whatever was going on. Ronan doted on Willow and would crush anyone who hurt her. As her best friend, I was within the circle of his protection. And Kade... well, he was something else entirely.

I glanced at the two men who were hovering behind Willow. My gaze skimmed over Ronan, drawn as always to his giant business partner. Kade Campbell stood several inches over six feet and was twice as broad as many men—although not Ronan, who was large in his own right. Kade's massive arms were crossed over a burly chest, his biceps bulging. A wave of comfort washed over me. While Kade and I disagreed on many things, something about his solid presence grounded me.

"Come here," he said, opening his arms. I stepped into them and laid my head on his shoulder. "I've got you." I melted into his embrace and let him support me for a few seconds. When I straightened and moved gently away, his dark eyes searched my face. "You're not hurt?"

"No."

Was that relief I saw in his eyes?

I forced myself to pay attention to the others and noticed Ronan quizzing the policewoman, who looked uncomfortable. Her expression eased as another police vehicle arrived and a tall, slim woman stepped out. She studied us all for a moment, her face blank. Recognition flashed through me. This was the same detective who'd helped with Willow's problem. I dug through my memories and found her name. Joanna Lee.

"Ronan," Detective Lee said with a nod to him. "I didn't realize you were involved."

Ronan held out a hand and she shook it. "Sage is a friend of Willow's. King's Security isn't officially involved. At least, not yet."

I frowned. *Not yet.* What did he mean by that?

"I'm afraid you'll have to wait out here until I've been briefed." She shifted her focus to the policewoman. "Let's go inside and you can fill me in."

"Yes, ma'am."

They headed into the house. I watched them go, a shiver running through me. Only the presence of the others prevented me from panicking.

"Tell me exactly what you saw when you got home," Ronan said, training his intense eyes on me.

I told him everything. By the time I'd finished, Detective Lee was re-emerging from the house, her expression carefully schooled. She walked over to us and stopped a few feet away.

"I'm sorry to tell you this, Miss Nichols, but it seems your roommate has been murdered."

<hr>

KADE

The hair on the back of my neck lifted, and I had the sudden urge to grab Sage and protect her from the ugly words Joanna had uttered. I could tell Sage was shaken, even though she was clinging to her usual serene facade. Her mouth was trembling and her eyes were a little too shiny—they gave her away. I placed my palm on her lower back, hoping she might draw comfort from the touch.

"She's dead?" Sage asked softly.

Joanna nodded. "I'm afraid so. In the bathroom. We'll have to wait for the coroner to determine the cause and manner of death but I highly doubt it will be anything other than murder."

Sage's eyes widened, and she curled in on herself. I wrapped my arm around her waist. "How long ago? Could I have helped her?"

Joanna hesitated. "Again, the coroner will be able to say for sure, but I'd estimate she's been dead for several hours."

Thank God. I hated to think how Sage might blame herself if she'd rushed out of the house while her roommate was quietly dying in the bathroom.

"You did the right thing getting out and calling for help," I told her.

Joanna's eyes flickered to me and then back to Sage. "Kade is correct. You acted exactly as you should have."

I got the sense her words weren't any comfort to Sage, and neither were mine.

"The crime scene team are on their way," Joanna continued, brushing a black lock of hair from her forehead. Her features were as inscrutable as always, with those near-black eyes and her flawless golden skin untouched by emotion. "We'll need to get a full statement."

I frowned. "Can it wait? She's had a shock and needs to recover."

Joanna arched a brow. "You know that it's important for us to get the details as soon as possible, while it's still fresh in her mind."

Frustration simmered in my gut and I pressed my lips together to prevent myself from protesting. I knew it, but that didn't mean I liked it.

Sage laid a hand on my arm. "It's all right." She took a deep breath. "Now is fine."

"Good. Let's go to the police station. Do you have a car?"

"We'll drive her," Ronan said.

Joanna agreed and we drove to the station in convoy. I sat in the back with Sage, who was frighteningly silent. She was usually so sunny that seeing her pretty face twisted with distress felt wrong. It made me want to hit something.

"You can stay with us tonight," Willow said, breaking the tension in the vehicle. "We have plenty of space."

"Thanks." Sage's reply was so quiet I nearly missed it. I barely restrained myself from taking her hand. I was glad she had Willow and Ronan for support, but a primitive part of me wished that I could be the one to watch over her and keep her safe. I'd given up that right when I decided not to pursue her, and I couldn't change my mind now. There was a reason I didn't date. I didn't deserve love, and especially not with someone as wonderful as Sage.

When we arrived at the police station, the driver paused out front to let us out, and then headed elsewhere to find a park. Inside, Joanna ushered Sage into an interview room and instructed the rest of us to wait outside. I didn't like it. Sage had been through enough. She shouldn't be separated from her friends. At the very least, Willow should be able to accompany her, but she didn't ask for any of us to go with her and I didn't want to be pushy so I reluctantly let it go. Ronan, Willow, and I sat on uncomfortable chairs and settled in to wait.

"Do you think Jessica interrupted a robbery?" Willow asked Ronan after the silence had stretched on for a while.

"Maybe," Ronan replied. "Did she and Sage keep any valuable items in the house?"

Willow scrunched her nose. "The most expensive things they had were Jessica's paintings. It's not like they had money or jewels hidden away."

"What about technology?" I asked.

She shrugged. "The usual. Laptop, TV. Maybe a few other bits and pieces." She hesitated, then added, "It seems more likely to me that either Jessica was in trouble or this is related to what Sage went through with her parents. Although, those men are supposedly all in prison now."

I stared, having no idea what she was talking about. Something had happened with Sage's parents? What was it and why was this the first I was hearing of it?

2

SAGE

I sat at a square desk opposite Detective Lee and another plainclothes cop who'd been introduced to me as Detective Hanson. Where Lee was a biracial Chinese American woman in her thirties, Hanson was an older white guy with a pot belly and a permanent scowl.

"Have you seen anyone unusual around your house recently?" Detective Lee asked. "Any cars that drove by regularly, or people you didn't recognize from the neighborhood?"

I thought hard. Having been part of a court case, I knew how important the little details could be. "Not that I noticed, and I'm quite observant."

Hanson cleared his throat. "Do you know if any of your neighbors have had break-ins?"

I shrugged. "I haven't heard of any. If I had, I'd have been more careful. But we don't talk to each other much so that doesn't necessarily mean anything. It could have happened and I just never knew."

He nodded. "Our officers will speak to them to confirm."

"So, you think this is a burglary gone wrong?" I asked.

"It's a possibility, but it's too early for us to have a working theory."

Detective Lee shot him a disapproving look, as if he shouldn't be sharing that kind of information. I sent them both a sunny smile, hoping it would ease her tension, but she didn't soften at all. If I was reading her correctly, proper protocol meant a lot to her.

"Did you see anyone in or around the house as you arrived home?" Lee asked.

I sighed, knowing I wouldn't be much help on that front. "Not other than the usual people coming and going. There's always a lot of foot traffic in that area."

Her lips thinned. "Was your routine today the same as normal?"

"Yes."

"What about Jessica's?"

I considered the question before answering. "Jessica didn't have much of a routine. She painted and went for long walks. Sometimes she'd hardly sleep for days and then she'd crash for a week. I'm not sure what she was up to today. She was sleeping when I left in the morning."

Hanson consulted his notepad, rolling a pen between his ink-stained fingers. "Did Jessica have a boyfriend?"

"Not exactly. She had an on-again off-again relationship with another artist." Their theatrics had been one of my least favorite parts of living with Jessica. They seemed to thrive on drama. When I found someone special, all I would want was to be at peace with them. As soon as the thought passed through my mind, I felt bad for having it. Jessica may not have been my friend, but she'd been a decent person and I shouldn't judge her. Especially not when she was dead.

My chest seized.

Dead.

Jessica was gone, her spirit returned to the cosmos, and I'd never see her smile again, or hear her painting at night while I was trying to sleep. I blinked rapidly against the rising swell of emotion.

"Do you know if Jessica had any enemies?" Hanson asked, drawing me out of my introspection.

I ran through a mental Rolodex of all the people I'd heard her mention over the months we'd lived together. "She didn't get along with everyone, but I wouldn't say she had enemies."

"Come on." Hanson leaned forward. "Someone wanted her dead. There must have been a reason."

My mind blanked. "Honestly, I have no idea. I don't think there's ever a reason to really want someone dead."

"Yes, well, not everyone shares your attitude." He passed me his notepad. "Write down the boyfriend's name and whatever contact details you have for him."

"He's not—" I shut up when he glowered and meekly wrote the information he wanted, then pushed the notepad back across the table.

"Who disliked her?" Lee asked.

I bit my lip, hating the fact they were asking me to point fingers. "Mostly other artists. Her paintings were popular, and people get jealous."

"Did she have any family?"

"Parents and a brother."

Hanson pushed the notepad back over to me and I scrawled their details.

"Okay." Lee folded her hands one on top of the other. "Now, I'd like to know if *you* have any enemies."

My mouth dropped open. "M-me?"

"Yes." She met my gaze coolly. "It's possible that Jessica was targeted because she lives with you. Or that you were the intended target." She looked me up and down. "Superficially, you resemble each other. Similar height, similar hair and eye color. Your hair is longer than hers, but some people might not notice that."

My stomach rolled. "You mean she might be dead because someone thought she was me?"

"Take a breath," Hanson said, his tone no doubt intended to be soothing but falling short of the mark. "It's only a possibility we're considering. Does anyone have it out for you?"

I inhaled shakily, resisting the urge to issue an immediate denial. I could think of three people who might want revenge against me, but they were safely tucked away in prison. Other than that, no one came to mind. I treated people well. I couldn't imagine anyone would hate me.

"Not anyone I know of who'd actually be in a position to do something about it," I said. "But I'm very active on social media and I have a blog and a subscription channel. Someone could have taken against me because of what they've seen online."

Detective Lee opened her mouth to speak, but the door opened and a uniformed cop appeared in the doorway. "Ma'am, sir, you need to hear this."

Lee and Hanson both rose to their feet.

"We'll be back in a moment," Lee said.

"Okay." I watched them go, hoping the door might be left open so I could overhear their conversation, but it clicked shut behind them.

To calm myself, I closed my eyes and envisioned a pond with serene waters, surrounded by lush rainforest. I imagined the sound of birds in the trees, and drew in slow, even breaths. I had allowed my mind to become scattered, and I needed to put the pieces back together.

When the detectives reentered, I opened my eyes and

offered them a small smile. Hanson's expression was thunderous, but Lee's was as stoic as ever.

"Something important?" I asked.

Hanson dropped onto his chair with a groan.

"There was a jailbreak yesterday," Lee said stiffly. "During a riot. We were aware of it but only just received the list of prisoners that are missing."

A lead ball settled in my gut. I had an awful feeling I knew where this was going.

"Richard Getty and Johnathan Baker escaped."

Oh, crap.

<hr>

KADE

The officer who'd been speaking to Joanna outside the interview room hurried past us as we sat waiting for Sage to emerge, his cheeks flushed and purpose in every step. Other officers also seemed to be buzzing with either nerves or excitement. Something had happened. Something bigger than the murder.

"Excuse me," Ronan called.

The man glanced over his shoulder, coming up short. Everyone here knew better than to ignore Ronan. "Can I help you, sir?"

"What's going on?"

The officer looked uncomfortable. "I really can't say."

Ronan's eyebrows shot up. "Do you know who I am?"

Under other circumstances, I might have laughed to hear him sound so high on the instep.

The guy squirmed. "Yes, sir. May I suggest you check the news online?"

Ronan inclined his head. "I will, thank you."

I grabbed my phone and opened a browser, finding

several articles that had been published within the past few minutes. It seemed there had been a jailbreak and someone had leaked it to the press. I clicked on the first article and skimmed the text. It reported that at least five inmates were missing following a riot at the nearby correctional facility. There were no names and the details were scarce. With a huff of frustration, I set the phone aside. I'd hoped the action might have something to do with Sage, but it would seem not. Still, there might be room for King's Security to become involved in rounding up the missing criminals.

When I looked back at Willow and Ronan to comment on it, my gut tightened. Willow's breath was shallow, her skin even waxier than before, and the corners of Ronan's mouth were strained.

"What is it?" I asked, disliking the fact I seemed to be in the dark about something.

"The breakout," Willow whispered, her moss-green eyes meeting his. "It was at the prison where the men who murdered Sage's father are being held."

Of everything I'd thought she might say, that hadn't even appeared on the list.

"I'm sorry, what?"

Willow searched my face, then frowned. "You don't know. I thought she'd have told you."

I clenched my jaw. "Told me what?"

"When Sage was eighteen, her father robbed a bank. He tried to run away with the money and cut his partners out of their share, but they caught up to him. By the time the police arrived, they'd killed him, but not before blowing out his kneecaps in an effort to convince him to tell them where the money was." Her mouth pinched. "I think they probably intended to torture him, but Sage knew they were there, so help arrived before they had time."

"Holy fuck." The contents of my stomach curdled. "She was there?"

Willow nodded. "Yes." She lowered her voice. "She's the reason the men were locked away. She was able to identify them so the police could track them down, then she testified in court."

"Shit." I couldn't imagine the strength of character that would have taken for an eighteen-year-old girl. "They didn't hurt her, did they?"

"No. They didn't know she was there. Her father had waved a gun at her and told her to run. She watched from the neighbor's backyard."

The poor girl. That must have been traumatic on so many levels. First to have been scared by her father and then to watch his partners accost him. Had she seen them shoot him? God, I hoped not.

"Where was her mom in all this?"

Willow winced. "Inside, unconscious. She'd gotten into an argument with Sage's dad. He'd pushed her, and she fell and hit her head. She died later that night."

Sympathy turned me inside out. "She lost both parents on the same day?"

"Yeah." Willow's face was uncharacteristically bleak. "It was a tough time for her. She had to go into witness protection until after the trial. She got out around the same time my dad died, so we moved in together." Her lips twisted wryly. "At least we were able to be there for each other."

I laid a hand on Willow's knee and squeezed reassuringly, but let it go before Ronan felt the need to glare at me. "I'm glad she had you." I wondered how to ask my next question without alarming her. I was sure Ronan's mind had traveled the same path as mine, and when I met his gaze, he gave a slight nod. "What did Sage's roommate look like?"

Willow cocked her head. "Average height, brown hair, brown eyes. Why?"

I sucked in a lungful of air and let it out on a rush. "Is there any chance she could have been mistaken for Sage by someone who hadn't seen her for a few years?"

Willow gasped, and turned to Ronan. "Do you think they might have hurt Jessica thinking she was Sage?"

He put an arm around her shoulders and drew her against him, tucking her under his chin. I made myself look away, feeling a pang of envy at their closeness.

"Maybe," Ronan said. "But let's not jump to conclusions."

"She needs protection," I growled. "From the moment she leaves this station, we need eyes on her."

Ronan nodded. "I agree. I've already emailed a request through."

"Good." I should have been relieved, but I wasn't. Uneasiness coiled around my spine. I didn't like the idea of letting Sage out of my sight for even a moment until I knew for sure she wasn't a target. Nobody else would be as vigilant as me, or as invested in the outcome. I *needed* her to be okay. "She should be taken to a safe house."

"I agree," Ronan said again.

Willow pulled a face. "Good luck getting her to go along with that. She won't like it."

I narrowed my eyes. "We'll convince her."

There really was no other option. Sage Nichols had to be protected at all costs.

3

The blood drained from my face and I was glad I was sitting down or I might have swayed on my feet.

"They escaped?" I asked faintly.

"Just the two of them," Detective Lee confirmed. "Parrish is still in custody."

That didn't make me any less afraid. Getty and Baker were scary enough on their own. At least I'd never have to worry about the other partner, LaMond, ever again. He'd been shot when the police tried to take him into custody, and died before he made it to the trial. But from what had come out in court, Getty was the most dangerous of the three—their leader—and Baker was his right-hand man. The others had been associates, the same as my dad.

I voiced my fear. "Do you think they might have done this?"

Lee looked grim. "We'll get to that soon. For now, can you tell me what contact you've had with any of the men convicted of killing your father since they were sentenced?"

"None." I knew hate was an ugly emotion, and I'd done

my best to forgive their past actions, but I'd be happy if I never saw any of them again.

"Have any of their friends given you grief?" Hanson asked.

"No. I had run-ins with a couple during the trial, but nothing since then."

Lee pursed her lips. "Did Jessica know much about your past?"

I hesitated, the question taking me by surprise. "No, I don't think so. We never talked about it, but if she'd looked me up, it wouldn't have been hard to find the details."

"I could be off track," Lee said, exchanging a glance with Hanson, "but do you think Getty and Baker could have mistaken Jessica for you?"

My throat closed over, and I clutched at it.

No, surely not.

I understood why she was asking, but that couldn't be the case. I'd been a part of too many deaths already. Mom, Dad, and Craig, the U.S. Marshal who'd died protecting me from Getty. I couldn't have another death on my conscience.

"Hey. Whoa." Hanson leaped to his feet and hurried around the table to rub his palm on my upper back. His hand stayed in neutral territory but I still didn't like it. Instead, I wanted Kade to wrap me in one of his comforting hugs, or for Willow's familiar scent to envelop me. This guy wasn't doing anything to stem my panic. Fortunately, I'd had years to develop coping mechanisms. I took a few meditative breaths and focused on picturing a golden light surrounding me. It brightened and grew, and the pressure in my chest and throat lessened. "I'm okay," I choked out. "Sorry about that."

"Are you sure?" Hanson sounded concerned.

"Yeah." I met Lee's eyes across the table. "Yes, it's possible that someone could have mistaken Jessica for me."

She nodded, and I thought I saw a flicker of approval. "At the time of the robbery, you were asked about the money. As far as I know, it was never recovered, and you claimed not to know where it was."

"I didn't," I said defensively. "I don't know why anyone would think otherwise. I was a kid. Dad wouldn't have told me something like that. I didn't even know he'd been involved in a bank robbery until after he was dead."

"I understand." Her tone was patient. "But you'd know better than most people how his thought patterns worked. You might be able to guess where he'd put it. And if I consider that a possibility, it's likely Getty and Baker do too. For guys like them, it's always about money. They might think you can find the money they believe they're owed."

A shiver rippled through me that had nothing to do with the temperature. Detective Lee's words made sense. It was only too easy to imagine that the greedy, brutal men who'd killed my father would be willing to do the same to me in order to get their hands on a prize they'd lost years of their life in prison for.

"That's enough questions for now," Lee said. She announced the end of the interview for the video recorder and switched it off. "I need to speak to Ronan."

I shakily got to my feet and followed Detective Lee from the interview room. Hanson stayed behind to sort out the recording. I watched Lee walk, noticing how graceful her steps were despite them being brisk. There was a fluidity about her movements that made me think she had a background in yoga or dance.

As we entered the area where the others were seated, Kade rose from his chair. He scanned me and his forehead crinkled with concern. "Is everything okay?"

I resisted the urge to fall into his arms. I was a tactile person and had never been ashamed of seeking comfort through touch, but I probably should be careful how much I relied on him when he'd disappointed me once before. I'd already leaned on him enough for one day. Instead, I schooled my features.

"Not so much right now," I said. "But it will be."

He cleared his throat. "We've agreed that you should be guarded at a safe house until the threat to your life is eliminated."

My breath stuttered but my response was surprisingly firm. "No."

He crossed his arms. "It's not up for discussion. Your safety is important to all of us, and we have the resources so we might as well use them."

I glared. "It's nice that you care, but I'll have to disagree. I don't want anyone else to be put at risk for my sake. You're welcome to investigate all you like and I don't mind staying at a safe house, but I won't accept a bodyguard."

<hr>

KADE

I pinched the bridge of my nose and tried to quell my frustration. Sage must see that she needed protection. We couldn't let her wander into trouble like a lamb to the slaughter.

"Sage," I said more gently. "I know you like to think the best of people, but whoever did this to Jessica is violent and dangerous. If they're looking for you, you need someone watching your back."

"Please, Sage," Willow said. "You didn't mind Kade watching over you when I was in trouble. Why not let someone protect you now?"

Sage gave Willow a look of betrayal. "All he did was accompany me to my grandparents' house. Besides, I knew the risk of danger was low. They were after you, not me. This is different."

"Wait." I struggled to follow her logic. "You were fine with having a bodyguard when you didn't think you needed one, but now that you might actually be in danger you don't want one?" She must know how crazy that sounded.

Sage arched a brow. "Believe it or not, I'm capable of defending myself."

I barely managed not to snort. From her expression, it was obvious she wasn't kidding. "You think the world is all rainbows and butterflies, but it isn't. Knowing a few self-defense moves won't stop anybody with proper training."

Her eyes glinted. "I may not approve of violence, but I'm not an idiot," she said tightly. "I've been learning krav maga since last year. I know how to shoot and I have a license to carry a handgun."

My mouth opened, then shut. That, I hadn't expected. Still, some of King's Security's clients had black belts in martial arts and still employed bodyguards because they knew they couldn't fight off every attack themselves.

"You'd be better off helping the police find Getty and Baker," she added.

I didn't reply. I couldn't deny that part of me wanted to track those bastards down purely so I'd have the satisfaction of throwing them in prison, but my instincts told me Sage needed to be protected, and listening to my instincts had kept me alive in the military, so I wasn't about to doubt them now.

"Actually, Sage, he's right," Joanna said, joining the conversation for the first time. "It's likely you're being targeted, so you can either take King's Security up on their offer or you can enter protective custody until we've recaptured the men you testified against. I'm not comfortable leaving you unprotected."

A range of expressions danced through Sage's eyes. Resentment and frustration, but fear lay beneath them. She pressed her lips together and sighed.

"Fine." Her shoulders drooped. "Somebody can guard me."

Relief filtered through me, but I wasn't able to smile when she seemed upset, so instead I got down to logistics.

"Which safe house is available?" I asked Ronan.

"The one on East Palatine isn't in use," he replied. "Take her there and let the office know to send some guys over."

Beside us, Willow hauled Sage into a hug. "It'll be okay," I heard her murmur. "I'm here for you."

I felt a pang, and for a second, I couldn't help wishing I was the one Sage would turn to when she needed comfort. Nevertheless, I was glad she had Willow. She'd need support to get through whatever came next.

4

———————

SAGE

I'd been backed into a corner, and I didn't like it. I hadn't had anyone to answer to for years. Not since the trial had ended and I'd been released from protective custody. My parents had been gone, and the only person I'd had left who genuinely cared for me was Willow. Since then, I'd worked mostly for myself—renting yoga studio space and teaching classes online—and nobody had been able to tell me what to do. Now a straightlaced detective and an overbearing alpha male were trying to change that, and it made me feel all kinds of unpleasant emotions I preferred not to experience.

I closed my eyes and leaned against the seat. Kade was driving me to the King's Security headquarters, where I'd been told we'd get some supplies before continuing to the safe house. He'd make sure everything was set up and then leave me with a protection detail. Willow had offered to come with us, but I'd told her not to. I needed to work through the negative energy in my head before it became overwhelming. Beside me, Kade was blessedly silent. I searched within myself, trying to identify the feelings crawling around in my chest.

Anger. That one was easy.

Resentment, too. Such an ugly emotion.

Fear. It left a bitter taste in my mouth.

But I also felt violated. I hadn't seen the men who'd hurt Jessica. I hadn't even seen Jessica herself. But they'd been in my home—my safe space—and they'd violated it with their evil actions.

I squeezed my eyes more tightly shut and released a shuddering breath. I sensed Kade glance at me, but he didn't say anything, and for that I was grateful. I drew in another deep breath and let it go. On the exhale, I channeled my energy into forgiveness.

I forgive you for forcing me into this position, I mentally recited, directing it toward him. *I forgive you because I know it comes from a place of caring.*

I tried to turn my mind to forgiving the people who'd been in my house, but I couldn't. The terror and grief was too fresh.

"We're here." Kade's voice was a masculine rumble. Some people might find his tone intimidating, but to me, there was something very warm about it.

I opened my eyes and blinked as they readjusted to the light. We were in the underground parking garage beneath the building that housed King's Security. Knowing the routine, I waited while Kade got out of the car and did a quick check of the surrounding area, then I swung the door open and joined him.

"We'll switch to another vehicle," he said, striding toward the elevator. "And we'll get you a change of clothes for tomorrow."

"Thanks." I was pleased he'd thought of that. My mind was too busy whirling to be of much use for practicalities.

Of course, I wouldn't be able to get my own clothes from home. My house was a crime scene, and everything inside it was potential evidence until the police said otherwise.

Kade pressed a button and we waited for the elevator to descend.

"I'm sorry," he said gruffly. "About Jessica."

"It was a shock," I said. "I don't think it's sunk in yet."

He nodded, and from his expression, I could tell he understood. Of course he did. He'd been in the military, and now worked for a private security company. Who knew how many acquaintances he'd lost over the years?

"I know you don't like the situation, but it's for the best." He sounded strained, and I glanced at him. "Your safety is important. I couldn't stand to see you get hurt."

Some of my anger melted away. While I might disapprove of the way they'd maneuvered me into agreeing with what they wanted, Kade clearly felt bad about it, and he had a big heart.

A snarky voice prodded at the back of my mind. *If he cares so much, then why didn't he call after that kiss?*

I shook my head to dispel the thought. His reasons didn't matter. What mattered was his actions. I needed to remember that. Perhaps it would have been easier to let go if I had more dating experience, but getting dumped shortly after losing my parents had made me wary of getting attached to men. It was unfortunate that the first guy I'd been wholeheartedly interested in since then didn't seem to feel the same way.

The elevator arrived and we took it to the floor Kade's office was housed on. He led me past an open plan area where several muscular men with unnaturally observant eyes sat at desks. We entered a storage area.

"There are clothes in these cupboards," he said, gesturing to them. "They're sorted by size. Get what you need for tonight and tomorrow, and we can collect whatever else we need later. I'll be back in a moment."

"Okay, thanks."

I opened the first drawer and saw a label on the frame that read "Extra-large." I skimmed down a couple of drawers until I found one with the right size and collected a pair of track pants, a t-shirt, and a hoodie, all free of labels. I assumed King's Security didn't want any identifying information on whichever staff wore these. I slipped the hoodie over my own clothes, glad for the warmth, even though part of me despaired at being clad in something so gray and soulless. I'd forged myself into a bright, strong person over the past few years and I hated the way the situation made me feel as though that was being taken away from me.

"Ready to go?" Kade asked from the doorway.

"I think so. Will the safe house have toothbrushes and other toiletries?"

He nodded. "They're always well-stocked and Ronan will have arranged for groceries to be delivered." He glanced at his watch. "We'd better get on our way."

I trailed behind him back through the building. We took a different elevator to the basement and Kade withdrew a key fob from his pocket and pressed a button. The lights of a white sedan lit up and he headed toward it. I waited for him to check the interior and beneath the vehicle, then I got into the passenger seat and clipped the seatbelt on.

I gazed out the window as we drove, feeling oddly disconnected. I reached into my purse and curled my fingers around the black tourmaline stone, my thumb rubbing over the smooth surface, allowing it to soothe me. I would be okay. I knew I would. I'd gotten through something that would have mentally damaged a lot of people. If I could survive that night eight years ago, I could survive anything.

After forty minutes of driving, we parked behind a

concrete block building located in a neighborhood of similar ones, all as soulless as my new clothes. Kade kept me close as we entered through the back and he guided me to an apartment off a dingy corridor on the ground floor. He slotted a key into the lock and silently indicated for me to stay behind him as we entered. The place was small and dark, with a living area that was multipurpose kitchen, dining, and living, and two matchbox bedrooms coming off it with a tiny bathroom between them.

I shivered. I didn't like the energy here. It gave me the creeps. I opened my purse again and found a selenite wand buried under the other debris, which I lifted out and positioned on the kitchen counter. I murmured a quick blessing under my breath, wishing I had the tools to properly cleanse the apartment of negative vibes; this would have to do. When I finished, I turned and found Kade watching me with a combination of affection and amusement. The amusement didn't upset me. I knew he didn't believe in the same things I did, and during our long road trip last year, he'd questioned me about many of my practices, but he'd never been disrespectful or dismissive.

"What's that?" he asked, gesturing to the crystal.

"Selenite. It promotes peace and calm and increases positive energy." I bit my lip. "I wish I had more. At home, I keep a wand in every room, but this is all I have on me." I would have loved to have some white sage to burn too, but I didn't mention that. Perhaps if we went out tomorrow, I'd be able to pick some up.

Kade just nodded. "If it's what you need, we'll find you more of it."

My insides flipped over. How was I supposed to keep my emotional distance when he went and said things like that?

"Thank you." I glanced around, needing to break the

tension before I did something stupid like kiss him again. "Do you mind if I have a shower?"

He went to one of the faded armchairs and sat. "Go for it. I'll be right here."

Warmth spread inside me. Somehow, his words made me feel safe.

Don't get complacent, I told myself. *You can't rely on him to keep you safe or he'll end up like the others.*

Another shiver tore through me, and this one made my skin crawl. I couldn't let Kade be harmed like Mom, Dad, Craig, or Jessica. I just couldn't.

<hr>

KADE

Sage was upset. She had every right to be, after what she'd been through, but I couldn't help feeling that I was missing something. I wanted to fix it, but I couldn't do that without first knowing what had caused the problem. There was one person who'd know for sure. I grabbed my phone and called Willow.

"Hi, Kade," she said. "Is everything okay?"

I glanced toward the bathroom, checking that the door was shut before I spoke. "Sage is more upset about having a bodyguard than I expected. Do you have any idea why? I didn't think she was the type to be impractical over something like that."

Willow was quiet for a long moment. I could almost hear her thinking. Finally, she said, "I'm telling you this in confidence. Please don't mention it to anyone else."

"You have my word."

She sighed. "When Sage was in protective custody eight years ago, her father's partners attempted to abduct her, back before they were caught. A U.S. Marshal intervened and they killed him. He was a father, with young children, and she took it hard. It's possible that's why she's so reluctant. She holds herself responsible for his death and doesn't want history to repeat itself."

I massaged my chest. My heart ached for her. Sage had seen more death than any person ought to. How had she emerged so bright and shiny out the other side?

"Thanks, Willow. I'd better go. I don't want her to catch us talking. Goodnight."

"Night, Kade. Take care of her for me."

"Oh, I won't be the one staying with her." I rarely worked in the field these days, and even if I did, I wouldn't want to be her primary guard. I couldn't be so close to her and still keep my distance. I'd done so well staying away from her, reminding myself every time I wavered that she deserved better than what I had to offer, and I didn't want to ruin that now. "My people are good. They'll keep her safe."

"They'd better," she warned.

A key scraped in the lock and I grabbed my gun. It was probably someone from work, but you could never be too careful.

"Gotta go." I hung up on Willow and aimed at the door. It eased inward and a King's Security ID card appeared through the gap, followed by a ropy arm and broad torso. I relaxed. "Grant. Good to see you."

"You too, boss." The bodyguard's eyes flicked around the room, cataloguing everything. "She's in the shower?"

"That's right."

"Great." He shut the door, locked it, and dropped onto a chair. "Do you mind staying to introduce us properly? I don't wanna scare the shit out of her when she gets out."

"Yeah, you got it." I stood, craving a coffee. "Want a drink?"

He shook his head. "Nah, not for me."

I went to the kitchen to make coffee for me and tea for Sage. Given the number of boxes of tea in the pantry, I could only assume Willow had asked whoever had provided food to send through plenty of options.

The shower shut off and I took my coffee back to the armchair and gave Grant a quick rundown of everything that had happened. Just as I was finishing, the bathroom door opened and orange-scented steam billowed out. Sage padded into the living area, wearing only a towel wrapped around her curvy little body. I stiffened, trying not to betray my physical reaction as I took in the miles of bare skin on display. She was pale and silky smooth, her body toned and shapely. And her hair... I gulped. All of that lustrous chestnut hair had been twisted into a topknot that left the elegant curve of her neck exposed. I felt a kick of lust. She was so damn sexy.

She's too gentle for you, I reminded myself. *She's an angel. You're a beast with blood on your hands.*

Grant made a sound of appreciation and I glared at him. He gave me a look that dared me to say something.

"Sage, this is Grant," I told her. "He'll be keeping watch tonight." I turned to my employee. "Grant, this is Sage Nichols. She's Willow's best friend and a VIP." With my eyes, I made it clear that she was not to be fucked with.

Sage smiled tightly. "Hi, Grant." She looked back at me and cocked her head. "You aren't staying?"

My stomach felt leaden. I thought I'd been clear on that, but she seemed disappointed. I hated it. "Yeah. Grant is one of the best though. You'll be safe with him."

"Okay." She fidgeted with her towel. "I'm going to bed."

"I made you a cup of tea," I said awkwardly.

A small smile curved her lips. "That was sweet of you."

She paced to the kitchen counter to retrieve the cup and carried it to the sofa, where she settled with her legs tucked up. My gaze raked down them. She had sleek calves and dainty feet with pale green nails. I recalled from our previous road trip that there was a small star-shaped tattoo on the inside of one of her ankles, but I couldn't see it from here. She sipped the tea and nodded approvingly.

"Do you mind if I leave the bedroom door open while I sleep?" she asked Grant, blowing away a few wisps of steam. "Will that be a security risk?"

"Not at all." Grant spoke confidently. "I'll leave mine open too so I can hear if you need me."

Envy speared through me. I loathed the thought of Grant being there for Sage when she needed someone to lean on, but I forced myself to swallow any comments. I'd created this situation, after all. I could have opted to stay with her myself. It would have raised eyebrows, but people would have understood, given who she was. I'd gone and decided to do the sensible thing, and now I had to deal with that.

The corners of Sage's mouth curled down. "I don't want you putting yourself in danger for me."

My heart squeezed. After what Willow had told me, I could understand why she was concerned about that, but I didn't want Sage to know I'd been snooping, so I stayed quiet.

"It's my job," Grant told her, "and I'm good at it."

"I have no doubt of that." But she didn't look reassured. In fact, she looked miserable.

We finished our drinks in silence, then I bid them both goodnight and left, ignoring the longing I had to follow Sage to bed and wrap my body around hers. To hold her close and shield her from the world with my body. But I wasn't her boyfriend—I wasn't even her bodyguard—so instead, I carried out a final sweep of the area and went home to my cold, lonely bed.

5

SAGE

I woke violently, bolting upright in bed, and looked around. I didn't know this room. Where was I?

But then my memory kicked into gear and I recalled the break-in yesterday, the interview at the police station, and coming with Kade to this dirty apartment in a rundown building. My breathing slowed, and I smiled wryly as it crossed my mind that when Willow had been in danger, she'd been whisked away to Ronan's penthouse, but there was no luxury for me, just this shabby hole in the wall.

I didn't resent Willow for it—not at all—but it seemed an accurate representation of how things seemed to go between us. She'd grown up with a doting father and everything she could possibly want, whereas I'd lived in everything from tidy suburban homes to trailer parks depending on how Dad's latest job was going. I'd never been quite sure what he did for a living, and in hindsight, I hated to think what he might have done to afford us the comfortable home we'd had when he was killed. Sometimes, I wondered if he'd felt like he had to resort to crime to make sure I had the best possible start in life. Would he have done the same thing if it had been just him and Mom? Had he agreed to the bank heist because he didn't know how else to get the money for me to attend the dramatic arts college I'd been accepted into?

The thought wiped my smile away and I rubbed at my aching chest. Whatever his reasons, he and Mom were gone. Now, so was Jessica. Possibly because of me. I just hoped it had been quick and painless.

My heart felt heavy and I closed my eyes and wallowed in grief for a few moments, but then I dragged myself out of bed and pulled on the track pants and t-shirt I'd collected from King's Security. I knew from experience that I couldn't allow myself to sink too deeply into despair or it would paralyze me. I'd had plenty of practice at developing coping mechanisms over the years. I needed to keep busy and channel my energy into something productive.

I pushed the bed into a corner, clearing a small space on the bedroom floor, and lowered myself to the ground. I worked through a gentle yoga flow, focusing on breathing and keeping an easy rhythm rather than challenging my body. Yoga could be as much spiritual as it was physical, and I needed to treat myself kindly today. When I was done, I automatically snapped a selfie and wrote a brief note to my followers, then I went to the door and peered through. Grant, the blond man I'd met last night, was seated on the armchair, a laptop on his knee.

He glanced up as I entered and smiled. "Good morning."

"Morning," I replied, a sliver of disappointment in my gut because I'd much rather have found Kade sitting out here. Perhaps it was for the best though. Being with me would only put him at risk. Although that said, I didn't want Grant to get dragged into my mess either. He seemed like a perfectly nice guy.

"You want to go for coffee soon?" he asked. "There's a

coffee shop on the next block over and I could use a pick-me-up."

I hesitated. "Isn't it dangerous to leave?"

He shrugged. "Nobody knows we're here. It's a big city. I doubt we'll run into any problems, and if we do, I'm prepared."

I gnawed my lip. The idea of venturing out made me nervous, but he looked like he'd been awake all night and he was the expert. He'd know better than me whether it would be safe.

"Okay," I agreed. "I'm not a coffee person but I'll come for a walk with you. Maybe they'll do breakfast smoothies."

"Great." He grinned. "Be ready in twenty minutes? That way I can have you back before it's time for a change of shifts."

"Will someone else be coming?"

"Yeah. Sean will take over during the day. I'll head into the office to report to Kade and then it'll be home to catch a few hours of sleep before we start all over again this evening."

I pinched my lips together to stop myself from making an unwanted comment about how he shouldn't be having caffeine if he planned to sleep in a couple of hours. He was an adult. He didn't need my commentary on his life choices.

I went into the bathroom and found the hairbrush I'd used last night. Brushing my hair could be a mission because it was so long and thick. When I'd finished, I left it to hang loose down my back and returned to the living area.

"You ready?" he asked.

I nodded, just wanting to get it over with. Grant patted his waistband, slung a jacket on to hide the fact he was carrying, and ushered me to the door. He locked it behind us and stayed close by my side as we exited the building. I glanced at him and noticed his eyes were constantly moving, cataloging the people around us. Some of the tension in my chest eased. Even if I didn't want anyone else to be put in danger, it was nice to be reminded that someone had my back.

We didn't talk much as we strolled along the pavement toward the coffee shop. I didn't want to distract Grant from his surveillance, and he seemed perfectly happy not to break the silence himself. When we arrived at the coffee shop, he ushered me inside and did a visual sweep of the room before guiding me to the counter. As we waited in line, I gazed out the glass door, keeping a wary eye on the people passing by.

The traffic was crawling, and I scanned the faces of the drivers as they passed the coffee shop. A black sedan paused as the stream of cars came to a halt—presumably because of traffic lights up ahead. I studied the driver's profile and frowned. Something about him was familiar, but it wasn't until he glanced out the window that I recognized him.

Richard Getty.

Everything inside me froze.

I didn't want him to see me, but I was scared to turn my back on him in case they noticed me anyway and came in. I reached for Grant's forearm and squeezed it to get his attention.

"They're outside," I said out of the corner of my mouth.

His eyes immediately flicked up and his expression told me he'd seen the same thing I had. He wrapped an arm around my waist and drew me close, burying my face against his chest. I circled my arms around him and leaned against him as though we were an overly affectionate couple.

"Don't move," he murmured. "They're moving on. I don't think they've seen us."

"What are they doing here?" I whispered, my heart

hammering like crazy. It couldn't be a coincidence that they were outside this coffee shop, could it?

"I don't know." He released me. "They're gone, and we need to get out of here too. Forget the coffee."

<hr>

KADE

I paced the length of my office, emotions boiling in my chest. Grant stood at attention near my desk, and Sage sat on a comfortable armchair in the corner.

"How could they possibly have found you there?" I demanded, directing the question at Grant.

"I'm not sure, sir. Perhaps they followed her from the house yesterday and have been tailing her since then."

I grimaced and rubbed my chin, the rasp of my hand over facial hair unnaturally loud to my ears. "It's a possibility, but that doesn't explain how nobody noticed them."

Surely, they weren't that good. I'd picked up no hint of a tail yesterday, and I'd been looking.

"It could have been a coincidence," Grant added. "We were in a public place, and it's a busy street."

I scoffed. "I don't believe in coincidences that big."

I flopped onto my chair, resisting the urge to kick something. Sage was supposed to be *safe*. What the hell had they even been doing in that coffee shop? Uneasiness rippled under my skin at the thought of what could have happened if she hadn't spotted them before they'd seen her.

Damn. I was never going to be able to let her out of my sight after this. If I wanted peace of mind, I'd have to watch out for her myself on top of the guards already assigned to her. They might not appreciate my interference—it was unusual for me to take a personal interest in a case—but it was the only way to ensure her safety. To them, this was just another job, but to me, it was everything. I was the only one who'd do whatever it took to protect her.

I gritted my teeth. I should have known better than to entrust the job to someone else in the first place. Offloading responsibility had never worked well for me in the past, and I shouldn't have let my reluctance to get close to Sage impact on my decision-making.

"Regardless of how it happened, we need to move to another safe house." I met Grant's eyes. "Go home and get some rest. I'll take it from here."

Grant paused, indecision on his face, as if he wanted to ask whether I was sure, but he wisely didn't. A pang of guilt flashed through me. However Getty had found Sage, it was unlikely to be Grant's fault. I should cut him some slack. But I couldn't stop imagining what might have happened to Sage if they'd been less aware of their surroundings.

"I'll see you later," he said as he left.

"So, what now?" Sage asked.

I sighed. "We need to line up another safe house. In the meantime, we can get you some clothes."

"Are you sure you have time for this?" She studied me with apprehension. "I don't want to get in the way of your usual work. I could just head to the new safe house myself. Like I told you, I know how to fire a gun and I'm trained in krav maga."

I gave her a look that let her know I could tell what she was doing. Seeing Getty earlier must have given her a scare, and now she was renewing her efforts to avoid having a bodyguard. I understood where her fear came from, but she needed to realize this wasn't going to go the way she wanted it to.

"Not an option. And to answer your question, you're not getting in the way. Keeping you safe is my number one priority."

She looked taken aback. "But—"

A ringing phone cut her off. She glanced at the screen and frowned. "It's one of the women I work with. Is it all right if I answer?"

"Go for it."

6

SAGE

I accepted the call and lifted the phone to my ear. "Hi, lovely."

"Hey, sweetheart." Toshi's voice was soft, with a slight accent. "I just wanted to check whether your friends caught up with you yesterday. They seemed eager to see you."

The back of my neck prickled. "What friends?"

"I guess not then." She laughed. "Two men came looking for you. They said they were visiting the city and wanted to see you while they're here. They were at the studio shortly after you left and I told them they'd just missed you."

My stomach dropped. Behind his desk, Kade stiffened and gestured for me to put the phone on speaker. I did. "What did they look like?"

She must have noticed something in my voice because she was quiet for a few seconds. "What's going on?"

"The men," I prompted. "What did they look like?"

"Middle-aged." Her tone told me she wasn't happy I'd avoided the question. "One was average height, the other short. Both a bit scruffy."

My empty hand clenched into a fist. "Did they give you their names?"

She huffed. "Some standard white guy stuff. John, I think. Not sure about the other one. Actually, come to think of it, I don't think the second guy told me his name."

Kade met my eyes.

"Is something wrong?" Toshi asked. "They were actually old friends, right?"

I sighed. "Not quite. Did they ask you for any information about me?"

"They said they'd just come from your house, but you hadn't been there," she said. "I mentioned that following your social media account is a good way to keep up with you since you update it so regularly."

I pressed my hands to my cheek, feeling suddenly cold. "Did you show them how?"

"Yeah. Although it seemed strange to me that they wouldn't already know about it."

I bit my lip, wondering how much to tell her, but I didn't want her to be at risk if they came back. "They're not good people, Tosh. If you see them again, don't let them in. Call the police. I mean it."

"I will." Toshi sounded shaken. "I'm sorry, I didn't realize."

"I know." She was as inclined to see the good in people as I was. "I've got to go."

"Whatever's happening, take care, okay?"

"I promise."

She hung up.

"I'll call Joanna," Kade said. "This could be an important lead. She'll need to question your friend."

I nodded with a sinking feeling. Yet another innocent was being dragged into this mess. I just hoped she didn't get hurt.

KADE

The call to Joanna connected nearly immediately. I filled her in on what Sage's friend had said.

"Hanson and I will head to the studio to talk to her as soon as I'm off the phone," she told me. "This is our best lead so far."

"Have you heard anything from the coroner or the crime scene team?" I asked, curious how the investigation was going.

"This stays between you and me," Joanna said cautiously. "You can discuss it with King, but no one else. Got it?"

"Yes, ma'am."

"It seems that Jessica was tortured before she was killed."

I frowned, then schooled my expression so I didn't give anything away to Sage. "How?"

She explained the girl's injuries, and my mood grew grimmer with each word. The men we were dealing with were animals. No one should be capable of doing that to another human.

"My working theory is that they mistook her for Sage at first," Joanna said. "When they realized they had it wrong, they decided to get as much information out of her as they could, which is probably how they were able to find the yoga studio. It was fortunate for Sage that they didn't catch up to her."

"Yeah." I broke out in a cold sweat just thinking what a close call it must have been. "Thanks for the update."

"You'd do the same if the positions were reversed." She paused for a moment. "How is she?"

"Doing well, all things considered. I'll talk to you again later. We're going to go pick up a few necessities."

"Watch your back, Kade."

"Always." I ended the call and looked up to find Sage staring at me with interest. "What?"

"Nothing." She shook her head. "Just thinking."

I was tempted to ask what she was thinking but I was afraid I might not like the answer. "Come on, wild child. Let's get you some more clothes."

I put my jacket on and escorted her out. We drove to the nearest department store and my head was on a swivel as we entered. If Getty and Baker had been so close to her once before, it stood to reason it might happen again. Every time she put more than a couple of feet of space between us, I itched to grab her, but thankfully, she seemed to realize how on edge I was and kept close for the most part. She chose a few basic wardrobe items from the racks and headed toward the changing rooms, but I stopped her with a hand on her shoulder.

"Don't try them on. I can't come in with you, and there are too many risks. If you're unsure of sizes, get one of each."

She pursed her lips. "That seems like a waste of money."

"We can donate any that don't fit to the office's supply for undercover operations."

She glanced at the changing rooms once more, then nodded. "Okay, but at least let me pay for some of them."

"Not necessary." I steered her toward the cashier. "I may not be a billionaire like Ronan, but I'm plenty wealthy enough in my own right. I do own a chunk of the company, you know?"

"That's right." She offered me a small smile. "It's easy to forget because you're so down to earth."

I chuckled. "Are you saying Ronan isn't?"

Her smile turned mischievous. "I'm saying his nickname, King, is well-founded. The man wears a suit like he was born in one."

"Far from it."

Her smile dropped away. "I know."

We purchased the clothes and headed into the parking building, but as we drew near our vehicle, I noticed a movement in the corner of my vision. I turned my head, almost imperceptibly. What I saw was enough to make my blood run cold. Within seconds, I had my gun in one hand and pressed the car key into Sage's palm.

"Get in the car," I muttered. "Quickly."

Her eyes widened but she didn't ask questions. She took off, surprisingly fast, and I swung around to meet the icy blue eyes of Johnathan Baker. The distance between us wasn't enough to mask the utter lack of emotion in those eyes. I was tempted to attack. Every cell in my body wanted to. But instead, I held the gun leveled at his chest. It would seem he hadn't expected me to notice him behind me because his weapon wasn't in his hand. A stupid mistake.

"Hands up," I ordered, hoping like hell that Getty wasn't sneaking up behind me.

Baker smirked, but he did as I said. Then, out of nowhere, one of the parked cars shot toward me, narrowly missing me as I leaped aside. I glanced back at Baker. He was climbing into the passenger seat. I bolted across the concrete toward our vehicle, launching myself inside the open door just as Baker slammed his.

Sage's eyes were filled with fear but she didn't hesitate as the engine roared to life and she thrust the accelerator down. Fortunately, I never parked where I might need to back out, because that could waste precious seconds when there were none to spare, so she was able to steer around a bend and down a ramp to the next story down. A loud crack echoed through the space and a bullet tore through the wing mirror. Another bullet pierced the rear passenger side as she swung us around a corner, down another ramp and onto the busy road.

I looked through the rear window. Baker was in the passenger seat of the sedan, gesticulating wildly, and Getty was behind the wheel. Sage navigated across several rows of traffic and turned off onto another busy street.

"Where do I go?" she panted.

"Just do your best to get rid of them."

Since I'd momentarily lost sight of Getty and Baker, I made a quick phone call to Ronan to let him know what was going on. A few hundred yards behind us, the black sedan turned into our lane of traffic. Sage executed a rapid turn, then another, and another. I kept an eye on our pursuers, but when several minutes passed with no sight of them, I allowed my shoulders to slump in relief.

"I think you shook them off." There was a multistory parking building up ahead. "Pull in there."

She did as I'd said and drove up to the third floor, where she squeezed in between a pickup and a bulky sports car. As soon as the engine cut off, she rested her forehead on the steering wheel, and I realized she was shaking. I rubbed her upper back.

"You did well," I told her. "You kept your head under pressure better than most people would have."

She raised shiny eyes to mine. "Thanks." Her mouth wobbled. "Can we swap now? I don't think I'm up to driving anymore."

"Yeah, sure." She was probably experiencing an adrenaline comedown. I got out and circled the vehicle. She stood on trembling legs and, before I could react, wrapped her arms around me and burrowed into my chest.

"Just a moment," she said quietly. "I'll be okay in a few seconds."

I held her close, burying my face in her hair and breathing her in. She was a curvy armful and I'd be happy if she stayed exactly where she was. Fortunately, she was thinking more clearly than I was and eventually pulled away. She swiped at the moisture beneath her eyes and hurried around the vehicle. When we were both seated again, I took stock of the situation. How had they found us? Twice in one morning couldn't possibly be a coincidence.

"Did you tell anyone where we were?" I asked Sage.

She frowned. "Of course not."

I pressed my lips together in thought. "Have you called anyone today?"

"No, but you know I spoke to Toshi."

She had. Perhaps they'd somehow been monitoring her phone.

"Have you been in contact with anyone else?"

She started to say no, but then stopped and her face fell. "I posted on social media this morning."

My stomach sunk. We already knew from Toshi that Getty and Baker were aware of Sage's online presence, and if she'd put up a post, there was every possibility it had included location data stored in the background. Many apps used tracking systems.

"Turn your phone off," I barked, annoyed at myself for not having thought of it sooner. "No more posting on social media. No more phone calls or messages. Okay?"

She nodded, seeming subdued. "I'm so sorry. I was on autopilot and trying to distract myself with work. I didn't stop to think it through properly."

7

———

SAGE

I stayed silent while Kade called Ronan to confirm that we were out of danger. I felt terrible for allowing myself to go on autopilot without considering the damage it could do. I'd been trying to avoid my feelings, and that was cowardly. I should have known better. And now, I'd put us both in danger.

My stomach cramped. I hated the thought that I was the reason those men had been able to find us. What if Baker had shot Kade? How would I have lived with myself?

Kade ended the call with Ronan and made another to Zeke. I listened half-heartedly to their conversation. It wasn't nearly as casual and friendly as his talk with Ronan had been. When he hung up, I glanced at his face and noticed he was scowling.

"Why does talking to him get you so worked up?" I asked. I'd already noticed Zeke seemed to rile him.

He flushed. "I'm not worked up."

I watched him steadily until he cracked.

"I don't know what it is about him," he growled. "I don't dislike him, but he always gets to me."

Interesting. "Why?"

He shot me a narrow-eyed look. "You sound like a therapist."

I managed a weak smile. "I've spent a lot of time with therapists, so that's not surprising."

His expression softened. "He's just different from me. Sneaky and slippery. I don't like dealing with people who aren't straightforward."

I could understand that. He seemed like a person who saw things in black and white, whereas perhaps Zeke was more like me and saw life in a million shades of gray. Nothing was ever as clear cut as it seemed. While I appreciated Kade's sense of right and wrong, it was flawed because nobody could ever truly know the circumstances someone else was facing. Sometimes, people did awful things for noble reasons, and vice versa.

"I get where you're coming from," I said. "But I don't know him well enough to comment." I pursed my lips. "I really am sorry I screwed up."

"I know." His tone gentled. "Just don't do anything else on that phone, okay?"

"I won't," I promised.

He started the car and reversed out of the park. "We've sorted out a new safe house. There's a town called Maple a few miles outside the city boundaries. Zeke has a cabin there that he's given us permission to use. If I know him, it'll be completely untraceable."

"You don't think they'll be able to find us?" With so many close calls, I didn't want to run the risk.

He sent me a quick, reassuring smile. "I may not understand Zeke, but I know him well enough to be confident that if he says it's untraceable, then it's untraceable. We just need to make sure we don't do anything to compromise it."

"Okay." I'd be super vigilant from now on. No operating

on autopilot or acting from a place of avoidance. I wouldn't make another mistake that might endanger someone—especially not Kade.

"But first, we're going to meet up with one of my staff to swap vehicles," he added. "This one is compromised."

"Where are we meeting them?"

"They're already on the way here. All we need to do is get to the fifth level." He navigated through the building, and it occurred to me that there hadn't been much point in us swapping positions, but I supposed that we always needed to be prepared for something to go wrong. There was a chance we'd be intercepted before meeting with Kade's contact.

But soon after we stopped, a vehicle pulled up alongside us and we quickly transferred our gear from one to the other. We waited for them to exit first before going our own way.

Kade seemed to know every street in the city. He never checked a map as he drove us out of the city center and into the more suburban areas before finally leaving Chicago altogether. He notched up the volume on the stereo, and I blinked in astonishment as the sound of waterfalls and rain-forest filled the car. I turned slowly to stare at him.

"What?" he asked defensively. "You've had a rough couple of days. The least I can do is make sure you have the music you like."

"But... you hate it."

He grunted. "I don't hate it. It's just not my thing. Especially for a long road trip. But if it brings you a little peace, I can put up with it."

My heart squeezed and the edges of my mouth lifted. "You are the sweetest man."

He scoffed. "Hey, now, wild child. No need to go saying things like that."

I angled my face to look out the window, smiling to myself. He might not want me to see it, but Kade was a giant marshmallow, and I loved catching a glimpse of his softness.

As scenery flashed by, I felt my troubles begin to melt away. Out here, everything felt like it would be okay.

It took half an hour to reach the town of Maple. We passed through a main street that lasted for only a few blocks. I spotted a quaint bakery, an old-fashioned pub, and a salon. We turned next to a convenience store and Kade finally had to consult a map to get us to a small cottage painted off-white in a sleepy residential area. Based on the homes around us, this part of town probably housed the working class but not impoverished. A small postcard lawn surrounded Zeke's cottage and a muscular Black man jogged down the front steps to meet us as we got out of the car.

"Reporting, sir," he said to Kade. "The place has been cleared and state-of-the-art security is already set up."

Kade nodded. "Thanks, Sean. Will you be staying on to watch the exterior while we're inside?"

"Yes, until nine," Sean replied. "Then Vic will take the night shift."

"Great."

Sean glanced at me inquisitively.

"Hi." I offered him a hand and a smile. "I'm Sage."

Sean grinned, his teeth bright against his dark skin. "It's a pleasure to meet you, Sage. We'll keep you safe."

My guts rolled sickeningly. I didn't want this friendly man putting himself between me and danger. My life had no more value than his. Or Kade's. But he looked so eager to reassure me that I forced myself to nod. "Thank you."

"I'll show you inside." We followed him into the cottage and he gave us a tour. It had a simple layout, with the front door opening onto a hall with one bedroom to either side, a bathroom beside the smaller bedroom, and a living room at the end of the hall, with a kitchen through a side door. The place looked like nobody had ever lived there, with stark white walls and only a few items of furniture. If not for the shopping bags on the kitchen counter, I suspected there would be no food or toiletries anywhere.

I shivered. Not only did it feel like nobody had lived here before, but like nobody *should* live here. It was a strange thing to think about an innocuous cottage, but I couldn't shake the feeling that something was off.

"I don't like it," I murmured to Kade. "It feels cold."

He slipped a comforting arm around my shoulders. "We won't stay long. I'll arrange something else. But for the moment, this is our best option."

Meaning we were stuck with it. I bit my lip. Perhaps I was being too sensitive. It wasn't as though I'd never been accused of that before.

"I'm sure it'll be fine." Especially after I'd burned some sage and lit some candles.

KADE

Once Sage and I were settled in the cottage and Sean had returned to his post outside, I sat on the sofa and called Joanna.

"Has King told you the latest?" I asked.

"You mean how they tracked you down?" She sounded distracted, but I wasn't surprised. A prison break was a lot to deal with, and the two convicts we were hiding from weren't even half the number that had escaped.

"That's right. I just wanted to make sure you were aware of their movements."

"It's good to have confirmation," she said. "Our uniforms are searching the area but they haven't had any luck so far."

"Let me know if that changes, and I'll call you if we learn anything else."

"Great, thanks."

I ended the conversation and pocketed my phone. Sage was still in the bedroom she'd claimed, and I couldn't decide whether to give her space or check to make sure she was okay. This whole day had been a shitshow and I could hardly believe we'd ended up here. I thought back to Grant and the way I'd dismissed him earlier, and grimaced. Hopefully I hadn't created any bad feelings that would affect the rest of the team. My guys needed to know I trusted them, and for the most part, I did. But I wouldn't take any chances when it came to Sage's safety. After all, I had firsthand experience with what could happen when you trusted someone to do something and they let you down. People could die. People in my life *had* died for that very reason.

I waited a few minutes, then paced up the hall and peered through the small gap between the door and the doorframe. Sage sat cross-legged on the ground, her hands resting on her knees, eyes closed. I backed away and made myself a coffee. A while later, she emerged from the bedroom, her eyes brighter than they'd been earlier and her serene smile back in place.

"Feeling better?" I asked.

"Yeah." She stretched her hands above her head, exposing a slice of her abdomen as her tank top rode up. "I needed that."

I just nodded. I wasn't sure exactly what she'd been up to, but it worked for her and that was all that mattered. I assumed she'd make a hot drink, but instead, she flopped onto the sofa.

"So, what now?"

I glanced at the clock. There were still plenty of hours in the day. "Would you like to learn some self-defense?"

"I already know a lot of self-defense," she reminded me.

"You can never know too much." I drained my coffee mug and placed it on the table. I was afraid she might be overconfident in her abilities, and if that was the case, it would be better to know it now than find out later.

I beckoned for her to come at me.

She shook her head. "I don't want to hurt you."

I refrained from rolling my eyes. "You won't. I'm former special forces. Go on, try anything you like."

She surveyed me cautiously, as though worried I might be setting up a trap. In a way, I was. But I wouldn't hurt her. I just wanted to make sure she knew what she might be up against.

"I'll act as if I'm going to grab you, and you respond." I moved toward her, reaching for her arm. She seemed to freeze for a moment, but as soon as my fingers looped around her forearm, she broke my hold in a well-practiced move and simultaneously thrust a palm strike at my nose. I dodged the strike, but she was already going on the offensive, grabbing my shoulder to get leverage so she could slam her knee into my gut. The motions were so fluid that I knew they'd been drilled in through hours of training. She stopped short of kneeing me and met my eyes in a silent challenge. I grinned. My wild child was full of surprises.

"Good work," I said. She was better than I'd expected. Nowhere near as good as me, but she might be able to hold her own against a standard thug. "What if I do this?"

I came at her again, and again, she defended herself. My smile grew. This was going to be fun.

An hour later, we both sunk to the floor, side by side against the sofa, breathing heavily.

"You're more skilled than I thought you'd be," I admitted, enjoying the press of her thigh against mine.

"I know." She glanced at me, and when I caught her gaze, I could see that she'd known exactly what I'd thought. "I've worked hard to be able to protect myself." She broke eye contact and leaned back, closing her eyes. I'd noticed she did that sometimes when she was feeling emotional. As though not being able to see me while we spoke would lessen the impact. "I should have started much earlier—probably after the trial—but I thought I was out of danger. Then, last year, we had those guys break into our apartment." Her throat moved as she swallowed. "They'd been told not to harm Willow, but they didn't have any qualms about hurting me. If Willow hadn't put herself between us, I think one of them might have raped me. I joined a krav maga class as soon as I could after that. I never want to feel so helpless again."

I slipped an arm around her shoulder and kissed the side of her head. "I hate that you were in that situation, but it's really admirable how far you've come."

"Thanks." She turned to face me, and our noses brushed. Her breath whispered over my lips, and a shudder tore through me. I wanted to taste her. To claim that pretty pink mouth and show her just how much I admired her with my body. Her eyes darkened, and her lips parted. We drew closer, as if drawn by invisible forces, but just before our lips could touch, she pulled away.

"No." She placed a palm against my shoulder and pushed. Her eyelashes fluttered, and I got the feeling she was having as much difficulty composing herself as I was. "No kissing." Her voice was husky. "Not unless you explain why I didn't hear from you after the last time we kissed."

My heart sunk. She wanted an explanation. Of course she did. I'd kissed her like she meant everything to me and then tried to distance myself. She deserved to know the truth. I thought even more of her for asking for it, but that didn't make what I needed to say any easier.

8

SAGE

I didn't expect him to actually answer my question, but to my surprise, he looked like he might. He shifted away and sat opposite me so we could see each other properly.

"I guess you deserve that," he said.

I gave him time to gather his thoughts.

"Here's the thing." He held my gaze for a moment, then lowered his eyes. "I think you're incredible. You're a good person, and I'm... not. That's why I stayed away last time. I realized once we were apart that you'd be better off without me."

I frowned. "I respectfully disagree. In my experience, you're a kind, honorable person."

He made a sound of disagreement. "I've done some things in the past that I'm not proud of. Things that make me unworthy of someone as gentle and warmhearted as you."

For a moment, I felt flustered by his assessment, but then the rest of what he'd said sunk in.

"Shouldn't it be up to me whether I think you're worthy

of being with me?" I asked, a bubble of irritation forming in my chest. It had been a long time since I'd allowed myself to be interested in a man—after Guy had abandoned me, I'd kept them at a distance—so his inexplicable reticence frustrated me. I drew in a slow breath and released it. "What have you done that's weighing on you? If you tell me, I can decide for myself how bad it is."

His face flushed, and he ducked his head, obviously embarrassed. "Trust me, there are some things you're better off not knowing."

I reached across the space between us and rested my hand on his. "This is a judgment-free zone."

He rubbed his lips together and raised his eyes again. They were dark and unreadable. "Maybe for you, but *I* judge me. I know you want answers, and that's fair enough, but beyond what I've already said, I can't give them to you."

"Can't, or won't?" I asked curiously. "Like, is it classified?"

"No." He shook his head. "Not classified. Just messy."

"Okay." I left my hand on his for another few seconds, so he'd know I wasn't rejecting him because of his decision not to open up. "It's your call not to tell me, and I respect that. But in my opinion, relationships need to be built on trust, and if we don't have that then there's no point in taking this further." I leaned over and kissed his cheek. "I'll be here if you change your mind. Any time."

"Thanks." He scrambled to his feet, away from me. "It's good to know where we stand."

I felt a prickle of regret as he sauntered out the back door, but I knew it was for the best. My heart had always been soft, and I needed clear boundaries or I ended up getting hurt. Besides, if we started a relationship, he might be distracted from his job, and even more likely to put himself on the line for me.

A phone rang, and I glanced around. It was the burner

phone Kade had got for me from the guy who'd swapped cars with us in the parking building. I rose and went to check who was calling. I recognized the number immediately and smiled as I answered.

"Hi, Willow."

"How are you hanging in there?" Willow asked.

I glanced once more at the door Kade had exited through, then turned and headed for the bedroom. I needed advice from my best friend, and I didn't want him to overhear our conversation.

"I'm doing okay," I told her. "We had a bit of a scare earlier, but we got away and everything seems safe so far at the new place."

"I'm so glad to hear that." She sounded relieved. "I was terrified when Ronan told me they'd found you."

I groaned. "That was me being careless."

"You didn't know." Her tone was stern. "I hope Kade wasn't hard on you."

"Not at all." I bit my lip. "He was nicer than he should have been, in fact. I *did* know better. I was just so eager to distract myself that I forgot."

"You like to work when you're having a bad time," Willow said. "You always have."

"I know. I just wish I'd been more thoughtful." I bit my lip. "There's, uh, something else I wanted to talk to you about."

"Oh, yeah?"

Despite myself, I smiled. Willow might think she sounded casual, but I could tell she was intrigued. "I never told you, but Kade and I kissed that time he escorted me to visit my grandparents."

"You *what*?" she shrieked. "And you're only just telling me now?"

"I was waiting for him to call and ask me out, but he never did."

"That doesn't sound like him. I'll—"

"It's okay, Will," I assured her. "There's no need to do anything. I don't hold a grudge, but I've often wondered what was behind it."

"So, is it awkward being around him now?" she asked. "We can arrange for someone else to stay with you if you'd prefer. It's weird that he's gone on a field assignment in the first place. I'm sure there's another bodyguard who can swap with him so he can come back to the office. Maybe Sean could come inside and Vic could keep watch outside."

"You don't need to worry. It's been fine. Nice, actually. I like being around him, and that hasn't changed. It's just that we nearly kissed again, but I stopped us and said we needed to discuss what happened last time before anything else happens."

"That was smart of you."

"Yeah, but." I sucked my lips into my mouth while I considered what to say. I didn't want to break Kade's confidence, but I also needed my friend's support and advice. "The reason he gave for never following up was something I disagree with. You know I'm all about everyone being allowed their own feelings and opinions and none being less valid than others, but I really think we could have something if he'd give us a chance. I just don't want to push him."

"Hmm." Willow was quiet for a while. "Did you make it clear that you're interested in him?"

"I'm pretty sure I did."

"If I know you, you gently told him your opinion and that you'd be happy to talk more any time if he wanted."

I smiled at how well she knew me. "Yeah."

"Then honestly, I think you've done all you can. Now

you just need to be there if he wants to listen. It was right of you to make it clear what you need to take things further, and the next move is up to him.”

Something inside me unknotted. “Thanks, Willow. I needed to hear that. Love you.”

“Love you, too. But no more leaving me out of the loop. I want to know what's going on. Promise?”

“Yes, I promise.”

We chatted for a while longer. When we said our good-byes, I felt considerably better than I had earlier. I was lucky to have Willow, and I'd never forget it.

KADE

As the day dragged by, I accepted that Sage had been right to call a halt earlier, but that didn't make it any easier to resist her. Everything about her drew me in. Her peaceful smile, her surprisingly steely spine, and her sweet nature. Not to mention those luscious curves, and the delicious scent that seemed to follow in her wake. Something earthy and natural but tempting as hell.

We made a trip down to the local shops to stock up on everything we didn't have, but we were pretty well covered between the groceries Sean had bought and the clothes we'd already purchased before leaving Chicago. Sage loved Maple, and I could see why. It was charming in an old-fashioned way. Wholesome and welcoming. The kind of place where I'd like to settle down if I ever decided to have kids. Unfortunately, I hadn't been able to give her leeway to explore today since we were supposed to be lying low, but if we didn't see any sign of Getty or Baker, perhaps we could venture out again later in the week.

She did persuade me to go with her to buy sage and a few of those translucent crystals she seemed to love. Then, back at the cottage, I sat and watched as she flitted from room to room, spreading scented smoke and chanting words I couldn't make out. I didn't go in for all that woo-woo cosmic energy stuff, but the tranquility of her expression as she carried out her ritual made me wonder if there was something to it. When she'd burned her sage, she placed a crystal in each room and played flute music on her phone while she did yoga on the floor. I watched her at first, but then I had to retreat to the bedroom because seeing how flexible her gorgeous body was made me frustratingly hard. I knew Sean would be vigilant outside, so I could afford to let my guard down a little.

I reached into my jeans and palmed my cock. It throbbed in my hand and I groaned under my breath. I tightened my hand around my erection and pumped. My hips canted forward. Damn, that felt good.

But then I stopped. God, I shouldn't be doing this. What had I been thinking?

I tucked myself away and attempted to recite the alphabet backward until I was soft enough to be able to comfortably do my fly up. I mentally cursed myself. I couldn't allow myself to indulge in this crazy attraction. I was sending the wrong message both to myself and to Sage, and it wasn't fair.

I went to the bathroom and washed my hands, then got my laptop out and decided to do some research. I'd thought I knew Sage reasonably well, but I'd seen enough over the past few days to realize that the carefree wild child I'd gotten to know during our road trip last year was only one aspect of her. There were other layers. Deeper ones. She was unexpectedly strong, capable of acting under pressure, and stubborn in a very nonconfrontational way. I wondered what else I might have missed about her.

I opened the file Zeke's team had compiled since we'd taken on her case, and started to read the summary. She'd moved around a lot when she was younger, and her father had been arrested several times on minor charges. Theft. Drunk driving. Possession of an illegal substance. He'd never been in serious trouble before the bank robbery though. The guy had probably gotten in over his head and not realized how vicious the men he was working for could be.

I read on. Sage had done well at school but wasn't a straight-A student. She'd met Willow in junior high and they'd spent most of their free time together. She'd joined the drama club and had backup roles in a number of productions. Her mother had changed jobs often, presumably because they'd moved a lot, but she'd usually worked for restaurants and cafes. From what I could gather, the mother had been the more responsible parent, squirreling away tips to cover the bills for whenever her husband next got caught up in trouble.

By all accounts, Sage's parents had spent the last few months of their lives fighting. The police had been called on one occasion, when a neighbor reported a domestic disturbance, but no charges had been filed. I hated the thought of Sage in such a toxic environment. She should have had love and warmth so she could spread her wings and shine.

Then the murders had happened. The mother's death may have been accidental, but if the father had lived, he'd most likely have been arrested for manslaughter. How much had it affected Sage to know that his actions had led to her mom's death? And for her to simultaneously have to process her father's cold-blooded murder and the revelation that he'd been a bank robber? It was a miracle she'd emerged out the other side with her caring nature and big heart intact. The trial couldn't have been easy either, and neither could the death of the marshal who'd been protecting her. Yet she'd made it through.

I shook my head in admiration. Sage Nichols was a very impressive woman. It was a shame I didn't deserve her.

9

SAGE

The next day, I was back into my routine of waking early for a yoga session. Usually, I'd livestream it for my subscribers, but I wasn't able to do that so, instead, I arranged the living room into the most aesthetically pleasing scene I could manage—which wasn't saying much—and positioned the burner phone I'd been given on the table to record.

As I fiddled with the angle, I had to sigh. I felt as though I'd lost years of progress. Once upon a time it had been just me and my phone, but I'd gotten used to having special lighting equipment, microphones, and camera holders. Oh well, I'd just have to make the best of a bad situation. I wouldn't even be able to upload the video myself, but Kade had suggested that one of the guys on Zeke's team might be able to post it in a way that couldn't be used to find me. He'd given me a phone number and said to call when I had the clip ready to go.

I grabbed a glass of water from the kitchen and sipped it, then checked my reflection in the bathroom and swiped on some lip gloss. I didn't wear much makeup, but using a little certainly helped me look less washed out on camera, and I wanted to appear as healthy as possible or else people might wonder why they were following my yoga routines and lifestyle tips. When I returned to the living room, I was surprised to see Kade leaning against the wall, looking as though he intended to stay there.

"Do you plan to watch?" I asked, a little uneasily. Obviously, I didn't have an issue with being observed since I shared my videos with thousands of people but having a gorgeous man a few feet away was different from the anonymous people online.

"If you don't mind." His dark eyes followed me, and my skin prickled with awareness. "I was awake and heard you moving around so I thought I'd join you. You probably don't want me in the background of your demo though."

My lips twitched. "Most of my subscribers are women. They probably wouldn't mind."

Mirth flashed in his eyes. "Did you just objectify me?"

"Sorry."

He winked. "Liar."

I grinned back. "You can stay. It's fine."

"Thanks."

"Just keep quiet. I'm about to start recording."

He saluted. "Yes, ma'am."

I smothered a giggle as I tapped the phone screen to start the camera and positioned myself in the space I'd cleared in the center of the room. I worked through my routine, pausing every now and then to speak to the camera. It was second nature to say everything I was doing out loud so people would be able to follow along without craning their necks to watch the screen. I did well, all things considered, but I could feel Kade's gaze lingering on me like a caress. Each movement felt strangely provocative, as though I was daring him to watch. To look at me. To *want* me.

But he didn't give any indication it was affecting him, and I was grateful for that. By the time I finished, I felt flustered enough without him contributing. When I finally switched off the camera and swigged more water, I was in need of a hot shower. Yoga was supposed to be calming, but with him as witness, I felt riled up.

"You done?" he mouthed silently.

"Yeah," I said. "I'll need to edit the video before it goes to Jonah though."

I started shifting the furniture back into place and he detached from the wall to help.

"When did you start teaching yoga?" he asked, shifting the sofa far more easily than I had.

I dragged the table into the center of the room and dropped onto the sofa, patting the cushion for him to join me. He did.

"I used to spend a lot of time at this shop where they sold crystals and homeopathic remedies. They taught yoga in the evenings, and I preferred to be there than at home. It was peaceful. The lady who owned the place knew a little of my background and let me take the classes for free. I only became a certified teacher after the trial though. I felt like people were watching me all the time, and since I didn't have many job prospects, I figured I may as well take advantage of the attention. I got certified and started teaching—mostly online, but a few in-person classes too. I also set up social media accounts and got sponsored by a few brands."

I glanced at him and found him frowning.

"Didn't it just make you feel more violated?" he asked. "You'd already lost so much privacy, and then you invited the world in for more."

I sighed. Yeah, it had been overwhelming at the time, but my life had worked out pretty well, and I was a firm believer that everything happened for a reason. "Before, people were prying without my consent. I turned it around so that I controlled the narrative, and I consented to what was happening. That was important to me."

"I can see that." His gaze softened. "You're a pretty badass woman, you know."

My lips curled of their own volition. "I'm not sure I'd use those words, exactly."

"I would." He was serious. "You're resilient. Far more so than most people."

"Well, thanks." I couldn't help but be pleased by his praise. "For the record, most of my subscribers don't consciously associate me with the tragedy of my past anymore. I'm just Sage, the person who teaches them yoga and helps them experience the beauty of meditation."

"You give them a safe space and make them feel able to express themselves."

"Yes." I shivered, surprised by his observation. I'd never have imagined him saying something so perceptive. There was more to this man than he let the world see. I only wished he'd allow me to glimpse behind the curtain.

I liked him. More than was wise. But despite my misgivings, I wouldn't change a thing.

KADE

I cooked pad Thai for lunch—one of the few dishes I could reliably make—and Sage and I ate together in the living room. I invited Sean to join us, but he didn't want to abandon his post outside. It felt strangely domestic to be eating a meal with Sage in a place that could be a cozy home under different circumstances.

"So, you were in the military," Sage said when she

paused for a drink. "You mentioned special forces. What branch of the military was that?"

"The army." I ate another mouthful and realized she was waiting for me to elaborate. I was reluctant to explain when everything I knew about her suggested she was a pacifist. "My team was sent in when we needed a covert approach. In and out. Maximum effectiveness with minimum fuss."

She nodded encouragingly. "So, you mostly had missions rather than being part of general combat?"

"That's right, although I did my days as a grunt too. Some guys are recruited straight into special forces, but that wasn't me." I'd come in at the very bottom rung of the ladder, but I wasn't about to tell her the circumstances around why I'd joined the army. I liked the way she looked at me—as though I impressed her—and I wanted it to continue. If she knew my past, all she'd feel for me was disgust.

"My sister joined the army, too," I added. Something I had mixed feelings about. I was proud of Audrey, but I doubted she'd have even considered the army as a career path before I enlisted, which made me feel doubly worried for her safety because if something happened to her, it would be my fault.

"Good on her." To my surprise, Sage looked like she meant it. "What's her name?"

"Audrey."

"Audrey Campbell," she said. "It's a nice name. Is she older or younger?"

"Younger. She's the spoiled baby of the family."

One side of Sage's mouth hitched up. "I have a hard time imagining a military woman as a spoiled baby."

I shrugged because she was right. Mom doted on Audrey, but my sister was by no means soft.

"How did you come to work with Ronan?" Sage asked.

I relaxed, pleased she'd taken the conversation in a different direction. "As you know, he used to work for Willow's father, Frank. Her brother, Tom, got rid of him as quickly as he could after he took control of the company, but Ronan had a lot of contacts in the security industry, and he was well-respected. He decided to open his own firm. He knew he couldn't do it alone, so he reached out to me."

She was listening raptly. "Had you dealt with him when he was working for Frank?"

"No. We, uh"—I cleared my throat—"knew each other from college, actually."

Her mouth formed an O. "You didn't mention you'd gone to college."

I grimaced. "I was only there for a year."

Until I'd trusted the wrong person, suffered a tragedy, and then done something stupid that forced me to leave. But she didn't need to know that.

"It's still more college than I've done." Her tone was wistful. "Before my life blew up, I'd planned to go to a dramatic arts college. I'd already been accepted."

"Why didn't you go?" I asked gently.

She sighed. "It just didn't seem important anymore, and I guess I couldn't help wondering if Dad might have gotten involved with Getty and his crew so he'd be able to pay the tuition fees. It was an expensive course, and from what I heard in court, Dad had only ever committed minor felonies before then."

My heart ached for her. I wanted to reach for her hand, but she'd established a boundary between us and I needed to respect that. "It wasn't your fault. He was an adult. He made his own choices."

She pulled a face that indicated she didn't agree, but then made a show of brushing off the conversation. "Anyway, tell me more about starting King's Security."

I wished I knew what to say, but she clearly didn't want to talk about it. "Long story short, Ronan and I agreed to pool our resources and work together, but I had a few months to work out before I could come on properly. During that time, Zeke reached out to him and, well, he has a very particular skill set that Ronan wanted, so he agreed that the three of us could go in together."

She frowned. "Did he ask you how you felt about Zeke joining?"

"Yeah." I pushed away my meal, no longer hungry. "I agreed to it. I'd already met him once through my work in special forces, and while he might not be my favorite person, he's good at his job." I scratched the back of my head. "We're lucky to have him. You won't ever catch me telling him that, but it's the truth. We wouldn't have scaled nearly so quickly without his help. The shit he can do with computers is crazy. It's just a shame he doesn't—" I cut myself off. "Never mind."

Curiosity shone in her eyes, but she didn't ask, and I was grateful for it.

"Enough about me." Time to deflect again. "What was it like growing up with your father?"

She fell silent for a moment, and I wondered if I should have asked something shallower, but I genuinely wanted to know.

"It felt normal to me, honestly. Like, in hindsight, I had an unusual childhood but back then, I didn't know any different. We moved a lot, probably because Dad kept getting into trouble, but I didn't know that at the time. Mom kept us afloat. Her name was Mary. She was the stable one. He was charismatic but unreliable." She nibbled on her lower lip. "It's strange. While I know my father wasn't a good man, objectively speaking, he was always kind to me. He didn't abuse Mom, and he didn't drink a lot or do drugs.

Sometimes I wouldn't see him for a while, but then I'd wake up and he'd be standing over my bed. He'd say…" She trailed off.

I leaned forward. "What did he say?"

Her small smile was somehow both sad and joyful. "He'd say that he'd missed me, and that he wanted to make sure I remembered that everything that was precious to him was tucked up in my bed."

My chest squeezed. "He sounds like a good dad." And what a mind fuck that must be, considering what had happened.

"Not good, but not bad either. He was just my dad. It's hard to reconcile that with the person who thought it was okay to steal hundreds of thousands of dollars of other people's money."

"Did you ever doubt he did it?"

"No." She twisted her lips. "Deep down, I knew he was guilty. Just like I know that Mom died because he pushed her. He's the reason she's gone. Even if they hadn't gotten into that fight, and she hadn't tripped and hit her head, she'd probably be dead anyway. He killed her the moment he tried to double-cross those bank robbers and cut them out of their share of the money." She lifted her eyes to mine, and they shone with emotion. "But I don't hate him. He was a crook and a killer, and it's his fault I'm in this situation now. But I've never hated him, and I don't think I ever will. If anything, I feel partially responsible for him."

"That's okay," I assured her, seeing that she was struggling to keep a grip on her feelings. "It's okay to have mixed emotions about it." Perhaps it was easy for me to hate him for what he'd done to her, but even I could see it wasn't that straightforward for her, and she seemed to be holding onto a lot of misplaced guilt. I shifted uncomfortably. I generally wasn't one for talking about feelings but something told me she needed it right now. "Whatever you feel is okay. It doesn't make you wrong or bad. It just makes you human."

She grabbed my hand. "Thank you."

I tried to look blasé. "It's nothing."

Her hand tightened around mine. "To me, it's everything."

My heart gave an extra thump. Damn, when it came to Sage Nichols, I was so fucked.

10

KADE

Later in the day, I headed into the small backyard and paced the length of it while I called Ronan. I was used to cramped quarters from my time in the military, but I wasn't accustomed to sharing my space with a captivating woman, and I was going stir crazy.

"Hi, King," I said. "Tell me you've got something."

"Unfortunately not."

"Damn." I'd been hoping they might have dug up actionable intel so I wouldn't feel so much like we were sitting ducks.

"We've got our best men working on it. Willow wouldn't accept anything else." The affection in his voice was clear, and I felt a pang of envy for what my best friend had found with Willow. They had the kind of loving, accepting relationship I doubted I'd ever have. They deserved it though. That was the difference. Ronan was a good man, without any shadows in his past, and Willow was one of the best people I knew.

"Appreciate it." I swept my gaze over the surrounding

area, making sure the coast was still clear, and resumed pacing. "You still think it's about the money?"

"Either that or revenge." Ronan didn't pull any punches. "If they think Sage can lead them to the money they stole, they're not going to give up on her. It might actually be better if they only wanted revenge because at least that way they might decide it's not worth it when they can't easily get to her."

I scowled. I didn't like the thought of anyone wanting to hurt Sage. Not for any reason.

"You haven't found any other angles?" I asked.

"No. The pathologist confirmed that Jessica was tortured and then her throat was cut. No hesitation marks, so it wasn't an amateur."

"Jesus." Nobody deserved that. Least of all a woman who'd been in her own home, minding her own business, when a couple of monsters attacked her. Wrong place, wrong time.

"Zeke has been ferreting around in security footage archives from eight years ago. He thinks that Sage's dad had the money on or near him when he was killed. He can't find any sign of it having been moved electronically and the videos he accessed show that he had a large bag in his possession when he was caught on camera a couple of miles from his house."

"I wonder where he put it." It couldn't have been anywhere obvious, or the police would have found it. They'd tossed the house and searched the restaurant where Mrs. Nichols had worked.

"He could have passed it off to an accomplice," Ronan mused.

"Maybe. But considering he was trying to cut his team out of their share, it doesn't seem like he'd be open to sharing with someone else."

"Splitting the money two ways is better than five," he pointed out.

"I guess so." But I wasn't feeling it. My instincts told me he hadn't trusted anyone enough for that.

"How's Sage holding up?" Ronan asked, changing the subject.

"Pretty well. She hasn't tried to duck out on me, and even during the car chase, she didn't lose the plot." It was unnerving me, to tell the truth.

"Let me know if you want to sub out. Nobody expects you to stay with her 24/7. If you were anyone else, I'd have already told you to go home and come back when you're rested."

I shook my head. I couldn't leave her. Not when I knew others couldn't possibly care as much about keeping her safe as I did. I was the only person I trusted to protect her. I'd shared responsibility for watching over someone I cared about once before and I'd been let down. I wouldn't make the same mistake twice.

"I'll keep it in mind," I told him. "Talk soon."

"You got it. See you."

We hung up. I dragged a hand through my hair and turned to see Sean doing a circuit of the property. I raised a hand in acknowledgment, and he nodded back. I wondered what he thought of my presence. It wasn't unheard of for me to participate in a bodyguard detail, but it was typically for high profile clients, and I usually wouldn't be present for more than a shift—just long enough to make sure any protection measures were properly in place.

Did Sean resent me being here? Did he think I should let one of the usual guards take my place and go back to my normal job? I sighed. Even the possibility of stirring discontent among my staff wasn't enough to make me reconsider my stance.

I returned my focus to the phone and found Joanna's number. After a moment's hesitation, I hit call. She answered after two rings.

"Detective Lee."

"Hi, Jo. It's Kade. Just wondering if there have been any developments you can share."

"Actually, yes."

My heart leaped. "Have you found them?"

"No, but men matching their descriptions robbed a gas station an hour ago. Hanson is on his way to the scene as we speak. He'll check the security footage and confirm whether it's our guys."

"Where?" I asked, desperate for information. "Were they armed?"

"Near Miller Meadow."

Tension eased from his shoulders. They weren't too close to Maple.

"The attendant said they had a gun," Joanna continued. "He didn't know whether it was loaded, but he didn't want to find out, so he gave them everything in the till and called it in as soon as they were gone."

"Smart man." I hated to think what might have happened if he'd resisted. These guys had already shown they didn't mind playing dirty.

"He was lucky."

I rolled my eyes. Joanna wasn't one to give credit unless she was absolutely certain it was due.

"Have you had any trouble?" she asked.

"Not recently. Hopefully they haven't been able to track us this time."

"Good." A voice in the background called her name, but she ignored them. "Let me know if that changes and keep your heads down."

"We will. Hopefully this robbery will be a useful lead."

She sighed. "That would be too easy."

I was inclined to agree. "Keep in touch."

A beep signaled that she'd ended the call. I slid the phone into my pocket and headed inside to give Sage the news. She wasn't going to be thrilled to know we'd be stuck here for longer. Neither was I, although a small part of me liked the idea of having this time with her. Her roommate's death, and the subsequent slipup where Getty and Baker had nearly found her, had given me an excuse to be near her. I knew I shouldn't complicate things, but keeping my distance wasn't as easy as it sounded. Not when my heart knew it wanted Sage, and the damn organ didn't care about logic.

SAGE

On Friday, after being cooped up inside for an entire day, I was desperate to stretch my legs. Even with good company, there were only so many card games we could play with just two of us, and I got the definite sense that Kade didn't want to talk more about his past. The few times I'd asked, he'd brushed me off, so I'd decided to just let him have whatever space he needed.

"Hey, can we go into town today?" I asked as Kade stood to wash his breakfast dishes. I sipped my green smoothie, wishing I'd thought to buy pineapple to give it a pleasant tang.

Kade frowned. "Do you mean Maple, or Chicago?"

"Maple. I wouldn't mind seeing more of it."

He rubbed his stubbled jaw. "It's dangerous to leave the safe house."

"But wouldn't they have made a move if they knew where we were?" I asked, appealing to his sense of reason.

"Not necessarily. They could be lulling us into a false sense of security so we'll make ourselves vulnerable," he pointed out.

I pulled a face. I hadn't thought of that. "Do you really think they'd be willing to waste time when they know the cops are looking for them and that their photos are all over the news?"

He continued to the kitchen and I padded after him, hovering in the doorway while he washed and dried his bowl.

"I'm not sure," he said, turning to face me. "But I'd rather not take the risk."

"Please." I pressed my palms together and pleaded with my eyes. "I'll do everything you say, and I could carry a gun. I'm licensed, remember?" I didn't like having a weapon on me, but I also knew the real world didn't always allow me to indulge my ideals.

He sighed. "I have a spare you could use."

"So, we can go?" I wanted to bounce with excitement at the thought of getting out of the cottage, but the idea of taking a gun sobered me.

"I guess so. But you'll have to do everything I tell you without question."

"I will." I met his eyes so he'd see I took him seriously. "I promise. Anything, as long as I can have fresh air and room to move. I feel so cramped here."

He shook his head with exasperation. "How did you survive in witness protection?"

"They had me staying in the middle of nowhere. I could go for long walks and it was fine."

"But your marshal came with you."

"Yeah." I felt a stab of grief at the reminder of Craig, the good-natured man who'd watched over me right up until someone killed him for it. We hadn't been close, but I'd liked him. He'd been kind to me, and he'd clearly loved his wife and children. He'd spent hours telling me stories about them. Then, because of me, he'd never gotten to see them again.

"Hey." Kade touched my arm. "Where did you go?"

I forced myself to meet his eyes. "Sorry, just had a bit of a flashback."

His dark eyes searched mine. "You okay?"

My heart squeezed. "As good as ever. But you know what? You're right. Let's stay here." I didn't want him to get hurt just because I felt restless. "It's fine."

"No," he said thoughtfully. "We can walk down to the main street. If Sean follows from a distance, he should notice if anyone else has eyes on us. It would be good to know for sure."

"But..." Images of Craig's lifeless body flashed through my mind. His blood had squelched between my fingers as I'd tried to revive him. I shivered. I didn't want that to be Kade. Right now, I felt like I was pushing him into making a bad decision.

"Come on." Kade slid an arm around my shoulders. "Go put your hair up and dress in something you usually wouldn't wear. I'll talk it over with Sean and we'll see what we can do."

"Are you sure?" I gazed up at him. "I didn't mean to be pushy."

"I'm sure." He brushed a kiss over my forehead, then let me go and gave me a little shove toward the door. "Go."

I hurried out and went to my makeshift bedroom, determined to follow his instructions to a T. I'd do my best to make sure nobody would recognize me. Thankfully, I had the kind of coloring and body shape that wasn't distinctive. A little short, a bit on the curvy side, brown hair and brown eyes. The only unusual thing about me was the length of my hair. I grabbed several scrunchies and gathered it into a loose bun at the back of my head. All anyone would be able to tell now was that my hair was long enough to be tied back. I went through the clothing we'd bought, realizing with a sinking stomach that it was all stuff I'd usually wear. Because of course it was. I'd bought it, after all. I opted for a nondescript pair of jeans and white tank top, which were plain enough that hopefully no one would give me a second glance.

When I entered the living room, Kade and Sean were talking near the doorway. Kade was still in jeans and a t-shirt, and Sean was wearing a sports jacket that I guessed was bulky enough to hide whatever heat he was packing underneath.

Kade was holding a gun, and as I approached, he turned the muzzle toward the floor and offered it to me. "Take this."

Reluctantly, I tucked the weapon into my purse. "Thanks."

"I hope you know how to use it."

"I do," I assured him. "I might not be a crack shot like you, but I can get by." I'd spent hours practicing at the range after our apartment had been broken into last year.

"Then we're good to go," Kade said. "Sean will leave first and scout up ahead, then he'll give us a chance to catch up and he'll trail behind to make sure no one else is following us."

I hesitated. "Are you sure it's safe?"

"No," he admitted. "But it will be a good test, and between the two of us, we'll make sure you're okay."

Fear wormed into my chest. Why had I even suggested this in the first place? I didn't want them getting hurt. I'd just been blinded by cabin fever.

"Maybe we should stay."

Kade came over to me and touched my shoulder. "Everything will be okay. Besides, you're not the only one who'd like to get out of the house."

"All right." That acknowledgment eased some of my niggling anxiety. If Kade wanted to leave too, then I wasn't being completely selfish. "Thanks."

He held my gaze for a heated moment, and I wondered if he might kiss me again, then he pulled away and headed back to Sean. The other man winked at me over Kade's shoulder, and I smiled in return. They were both such good guys.

Sean vanished through the back door. I made to follow him, but Kade gestured for me to wait. A couple of minutes later, his phone buzzed, and he guided me through the door and locked it behind us. He stayed close to me as we walked around the cottage and onto the street. He was a hulking form at my side, his massive arm brushing mine every few steps. I felt positively tiny beside him.

I glanced at his hand, which swung near his hip, his fingers loosely curled as though he was prepared for combat at any second. It was a strong hand. Large and capable. I'd have liked to slip mine into it, but I didn't want to do anything that might distract him. I was quiet while we walked, determined to make sure nothing I did would take Kade's mind off the task at hand. I felt bad enough that we were outside. The least I could do was make sure I didn't interfere with his ability to do his job.

I caught a few glimpses of Sean up ahead but then he disappeared. His ability to vanish like that unnerved me, and I was relieved he was on our side and not the other. Kade checked his phone a couple of times—presumably Sean was sending him updates—but he didn't mention them to me. I had the urge to hum to break the silence, but if I did that, it might cover sounds that would alert Kade to danger.

I was pleased I'd chosen to wear sneakers because it was further to the main street than I remembered. We only passed a few people on the way, and I was grateful to see more up ahead as we approached the shops. I looked through the window of a small convenience store as we drew level with it but continued walking. We encountered a post office, a gift store, and a cafe. Then I broke into a grin at the sight of a poky building with a purple sign reading "Atlantis" above the doorway.

"Can we go in there?" I asked, already eager to check out the clusters of crystals I could see through the windows.

Kade stepped up beside me and raised a hand to shield his eyes while he scanned the inside of the store. "Yeah, but stay close."

"I will." I bounced into the store, something inside me instantly soothing as the soft melody playing through the speakers washed over me. I went straight to the display of semi-precious stones. They shone beautifully and each was labeled with a handwritten note that identified the crystal and its properties. I explored the entire collection, which included some I hadn't seen before, and picked up a pair of selenite crystals, then turned to look around the rest of the shop. I gasped as I noticed the wall of tea leaves opposite. I drank them up greedily with my eyes. So many flavors. I didn't know where to look first.

"Would you like to try some?" a voice asked from behind us.

I turned and spotted a woman with long gray hair. She smiled at me warmly. "That would be lovely."

"Any preferences?" she asked.

I scanned the options again. "Can I try the ginger chai please?"

"Absolutely." She went behind the counter and made a small sample cup of the tea.

When she passed it over, I blew across the surface and then sipped. "Oh, wow. That's so good."

She beamed. "I'm glad you like it. Are there any others you'd like to taste?"

Fifteen minutes later, I emerged from the shop with five new boxes of tea, two selenite crystals, and a big smile. I carried my purchases and stayed in step with Kade while he backtracked to the coffee shop. I waited near the door while he ordered, and then we returned to the cottage together.

I stole a look at Kade's rugged features as we walked and felt a pang in my chest. This seemed like something a couple would do together. Not for the first time, I wished he'd called after our kiss last year, but then I reminded myself that regret was pointless. We were sharing a moment now, and that was exactly as it should be. I just hoped there would be only good karma flowing to me from now on.

11

———

SAGE

After our shopping expedition, the rest of the day flew by. Instead of feeling cooped up, I was excited to charge the crystals and set them out, and to brew tea for myself, Sean, and Kade. I composed a blog post and forwarded it to Jonah, from Zeke's team, to upload on my behalf. Then, later in the evening, just as I was beginning to grow hungry, Sean popped inside to let us know he was leaving. His replacement had arrived and, based on the smells wafting in, he'd brought dinner. My stomach growled as I waved goodbye to Sean and went to make sure we had plates and cutlery.

The overnight guard, Vic, carried in a selection of Chinese food. We exchanged a few words of small talk while he dished himself a meal but he brushed off my invitation to join us. Kade and I sat cross-legged on the floor and dug in. If I was hungry, Kade seemed to be ravenous, and I realized we'd had snacks but no real lunch. I'd have to cook something tomorrow so it wouldn't happen again.

"So, what were you studying in college when you met Ronan?" I asked as we ate, hoping he might be open to sharing a little more with me after a lovely day.

A shadow seemed to pass over his face, but it was gone so quickly I wondered if I'd imagined it. He scooped more fried noodles onto his plate. "Criminal law."

My jaw dropped. "You were going to be a lawyer?"

He shrugged. "It was an option. I wanted to work in the justice system and make some improvements. In hindsight, I was naive."

"But still, that's a very honorable goal."

I tried to picture Kade as a lawyer, wearing a suit and standing in court. I couldn't see it. He was too raw for that. Lawyers always seemed to have a shiny outer shell, and Kade was just his rugged, authentic self.

"So, why did you change your mind?" I asked, dunking a wonton in sweet and sour sauce.

He stiffened. "Circumstances. It didn't work out." From his tone, it was clear the topic was off-limits. "When did you become friends with Willow?"

I hid a smile at his diversionary tactic. "I must have been about twelve or so. Some kids at school were teasing Willow because of her name. I stood up for her, and we became friends. Of course, after that, people mocked *both* of our names."

"Kids can be cruel."

"I know, but it didn't really bother me. I just hated seeing her upset." I'd always been better at letting things roll off my shoulders than Willow had. "We stayed friends through everything, although sometimes we went a while without seeing each other. Distance has never been a problem for us. We have one of those friendships that can withstand anything."

When he didn't immediately reply, I looked up and found him watching me so intensely that I shivered. There was something in his dark gaze that unsettled me, but not in a bad way. For some reason, I liked having his full attention. I wanted more of it.

"Did you know I still own the house where it all happened?" I blurted out. My cheeks heated. I had no idea what had prompted me to say it, but the confession hung awkwardly in the air between us.

Kade's eyebrows knitted together. "Do you mean the place where your father was shot?"

I pressed my lips together and pushed away my plate, suddenly no longer hungry. "Yes. They left it to me in the will, but it was tied up in red tape for years. I received a letter a little while ago to let me know I could finally do whatever I wanted with it, but I haven't been back there yet. I can't seem to bring myself to face it."

"It must hold a lot of memories for you."

"It does. Sometimes I think I hate it." I'd worked so hard to clear away the emotional entanglements from that time in my life, but there were some things that even years of therapy and a positive mindset couldn't erase. I wiped my hands on a napkin and forced myself to smile, relieved he didn't push for more information. "Will you let me read your palm?"

He narrowed his eyes. I could tell he wanted to refuse—he'd made it clear he didn't believe in anything even vaguely mystical—but he nodded. "Yeah, why not?" He wiped his own hands on a napkin and offered me the right one.

"Can I have the other too?" I prompted, and he reluctantly turned the left palm-up as well. I studied them both carefully. "You have earth hands, which means you're practical and grounded."

"I could have told you that," he muttered, but quieted when I shot him a look.

I cupped his right hand in mine first, smoothing my fingers over the mounds and planes, tracing the creases. A flare of heat reminded me of how I'd admired his large hands earlier, and I squirmed.

"You have a long love line, and a clear head line," I observed. "Indicators of good emotional health and intelligence." Out of curiosity, I looked at his marriage line. One line, clear and unbroken. Something in my stomach swooped as I fought the urge to compare it to my own, which I already knew to be nearly identical. I released his hand. "Anyway, that's that."

"No predictions for the future?" he asked gruffly.

"Nope." At least none that I wanted to risk saying aloud in case I jinxed them. "Come on, we'd better clean up."

KADE

Hours later, I still couldn't shake the memory of how Sage's delicate fingertips had felt skimming over my palm. The entire experience had been strangely intimate. Neither of us had crossed any boundaries, and it had been innocent, but her light touch had stirred me in a way nothing had in a long time. I wanted more of it. I ached for her to run those gentle fingers over the rest of my body.

I groaned and pushed off the sofa to head outside and speak to Vic. Sage had showered and gone to bed a while ago, but I was too wired to sleep.

"Hey, Vic," I said as I jogged down the porch stairs. He was leaning against the fence, deceptively relaxed, but I knew he could have any intruder on the ground within seconds. The guy was good. I only hired the best—even if I sometimes had a hard time trusting them. Most of my men were former military or ex-cops, but occasionally I'd take on someone from a different background. Vic was a retired professional MMA fighter. He'd earned enough during his previous career that he no longer needed to work, but he claimed to get bored without something to give him purpose, and he made an imposing bodyguard.

"Sir." He nodded respectfully.

"Any movement?"

"Not a peep." He took a cigarette from his pocket and lit up.

"Good." I leaned against the fence upwind of him so his cigarette smoke wouldn't blow into my face. I didn't mind the smell of it, but I'd rather not breathe in too much. "Hope you got plenty of rest today." Our usual night guard had had a family emergency, so Vic had been pulled off another case to cover for him.

"Enough." He puffed on the cigarette. Like me, Vic wasn't one for lots of words. He waved toward the house. "She's cute. She single?"

A growl tore from my throat, and he looked at me in alarm.

"Sorry, man." He held his hands out in a gesture of peace. "Didn't realize it was like that."

"Like *what*?" I snapped, irritated that he'd read something into my response. "She's a client."

"Not a proper one, though," he pointed out. "This case is personal. She's not paying for our services, is she?"

"No," I admitted.

"Then what's the big deal?"

I glared at him, but in the dark, he didn't seem to notice. "She's... we're..." How could I explain the fact I liked Sage a whole hell of a lot but didn't plan to act on it because of shit in my past? "It's complicated."

He smirked. "Isn't it always?"

I cleared my throat. "How's the Michelangelo project going?"

The Michelangelo project was a case we'd been asked to

look into on behalf of a wealthy client who'd had several pieces of art stolen. There was rumored to be a team of top-notch, high-end art thieves pulling off heists in Chicago and the surrounding area, but they'd supposedly been targeting the kind of people who didn't like to report thefts since the goods stolen from them had often been stolen from someone else to begin with. Unfortunately for the thieves, they'd miscalculated this time and our client had come forward.

Vic winced. "Still not a lot to show. I've been asking questions about the underground art scene, but nobody is talking."

"Damn. Does the client know?"

"Yeah, and he wants us to keep going. I think they hurt his pride when they broke through that supposedly impenetrable security system he had, so he doesn't care how much money he has to throw at us to bring them in."

"Good for us, I guess. What else is new?"

Vic and I chatted for a while longer before I returned inside. I brushed my teeth and lingered outside Sage's bedroom, needing to know she was safe but not wanting to disturb her. Eventually, I eased the door open just enough to see inside. She lay curled on her side, her eyes closed, her lips slightly parted. Everything in me stilled. God, I wished I could cross over to her and drop a kiss on her cheek, then climb into bed beside her and cuddle her close. She let out a soft sigh and my heart gave a *rat-a-tat-tat*. She was so beautiful. So sweet despite everything that had happened to her. That took true strength.

I backed away and closed the door. I rested my forehead against the wood and gritted my teeth. I was all tied up in knots over Sage and I couldn't even bring myself to care.

12

KADE

My phone rang while Sage was going through her morning yoga routine. I answered it and stepped into the kitchen, grateful for the distraction. Every time I watched Sage's graceful movements, I felt more like there was a beast inside me, desperate to break free. One of these days, I'd snap and bend her wonderfully flexible body over the couch and kiss her senseless.

I clenched my free hand into a fist and barked, "Yeah?"

"Kade?" It was Ronan. "How's everything going?"

"No sightings of Getty or Baker," I replied. "No other trouble either. I think we've given them the slip."

"Glad to hear it." He spoke briskly. "Joanna and Hanson interrogated Raymond Parrish yesterday evening."

I frowned. "The other guy who was involved in the murder of Sage's father?"

"That's right," he confirmed. "He didn't give up any useful information. Joanna suspects he knew about the jailbreak and was supposed to be part of it, but he got caught up in the riot and wasn't able to get away. If that's the case, it's possible he thinks Getty and Baker will get the money and come back for him."

I considered that. "Did the cops try to make him question their loyalty?"

"According to Jo, they gave it a shot, but he wasn't buying their story."

"Damn it." If Parrish remained loyal to his co-conspirators, we wouldn't get anything out of him. "Are we allowed to talk to him?"

"Yes." There was a smile in his voice. "We've been approved to have a conversation with Parrish later this morning."

"I want to be there."

"I thought you might. Are you comfortable leaving Sage with Sean, or would you prefer to have another bodyguard sent out as well?"

I felt a pang of frustration. I didn't want to leave Sage with someone else, even for a few hours, but I knew logically that she'd be fine. It was just a deep-seated mistrust of the world that made me want to see to her needs personally. I gritted my teeth. It wasn't fair to treat my team as if I didn't trust them. It must impact their confidence—both in themselves and in me as a boss. But damn, I didn't want Sage to leave my sight.

I forced myself to say, "Sean will be fine."

"Great. I'll text you the details. See you there."

"Thanks, King." We ended the call. I pocketed my phone and turned to find Sage standing in the doorway. "I didn't realize you'd finished."

"I was curious who was calling," she said. "Any news?"

I hesitated, debating how much to tell her. "The police questioned Parrish, but he wasn't able to give them any useful information, so King and I are going to see if we can do any better."

She raised her chin. "I want to be there."

"No." I should have seen this coming. She didn't like taking a back seat. "It's too dangerous. We need to leave you here with Sean, where you're safe."

Her expression grew determined. "You weren't involved in the original case. No matter how much you read the files, you can't possibly know as much about it as I do. I can offer insights that no one else has."

My jaw clenched involuntarily. She had a point.

"Call Ronan," she said. "Tell him what I said and ask if I can come. Please," she added as an afterthought.

I scowled. I didn't want to take Sage into a prison. They were sordid, dirty places—not the kind of environment she should ever be exposed to. But it also wasn't my job to make that decision. She might be a client of sorts, but she could easily decide she'd rather have police protection and I didn't trust anyone else to be in charge of her welfare.

"Give me a sec." I grabbed my phone, found Ronan's number, and called him back. "Sage wants to come," I said when he answered. "She says she might have insight into Parrish that we don't."

"Damn, she's right." Ronan sounded as frustrated as I felt. "Bring her. But be very careful. Double-check everything. If Sage gets hurt, Willow will kill me."

"You got it, boss man." I hung up and eyeballed Sage. "You're to do exactly what I say, when I say it. No arguing. No delaying. You hear me?"

She nodded. "You're the expert."

I huffed in gratification. "Damn right I am. All right, come on, before I change my mind."

She grinned and hurried out of the kitchen, leaving me alone with my doubts. This was a terrible idea. I just hoped we weren't compromising Sage's hard-won safety.

When I strode back into the living room, Sage had her purse on her lap and had donned a sweater.

I crooked an eyebrow. "Ready to go?"

She nodded.

"Okay, I'll just be a moment."

I packed my gun and a couple of backup knives, then shoved a few items into an emergency go-bag in case we had to run and couldn't return to the cottage. I made sure to add a change of clothes for Sage, then jerked my head toward the door. Outside, I explained the situation to Sean, who agreed to stay at the cottage to ensure nobody broke in while we were gone. I unlocked the car and checked the underside and the interior for explosive devices before giving Sage the go-ahead to get in. As we pulled away from the curb, I had a bad feeling in my gut. Something was going to go wrong.

SAGE

The prison was a tall triangular building with walls the color of sand and disturbingly small windows. As we approached, I couldn't help but feel sorry for the people trapped inside. They may be criminals, but did anyone deserve to be shut away in a place like that and forgotten?

Kade parked on the side of the street and we walked the short distance to the entrance. I shivered and unconsciously reached for his hand. It felt as though the walls themselves were drenched with human misery. He gave my hand a quick squeeze but then let it go to guide me through the first layer of security.

The interior of the jail was just as grim as the exterior, with blanched walls and hard-faced staff who seemed to speak only when necessary and never with kindness. I shrunk in on myself and stuck close to Kade, experiencing a pang of regret at insisting on coming with him.

While he explained why we were there to a receptionist, I closed my eyes, breathed in through my nose and imagined a shining white aura around myself, keeping me safe from the negative energy beating in at us. I opened my eyes when Kade touched my elbow, and he escorted me through another layer of security to a room with several small, rectangular tables that were bolted to the ground. Ronan sat behind one of them. There was a chair beside him and another a few feet away.

"You take this one," Kade said, indicating the one further away. He sunk onto the one beside Ronan and they exchanged a few words of greeting.

"They'll be getting Parrish now," Ronan said. "I asked them to wait until you arrived."

"Thanks," Kade replied.

Ronan turned to Sage. "How are you holding up?"

She waved a hand back and forth. "Been better, been worse."

"Well, hopefully it'll all be over soon."

Hopefully. But he didn't sound convinced and neither was I.

The door opened and a thickset man with a scraggly beard and thinning hair was marched into the room, his wrists cuffed together. Even though I'd spent hours in court with Raymond Parrish, I almost wouldn't have recognized him if I didn't know who he was. He'd bulked up and looked even less hygienic than before. I supposed prison brought out the worst in people. He surveyed the room, his head back defiantly, and skimmed over me, but then something flickered across his face and his attention snapped back to me. His mouth curled in a nasty sneer. I tried to picture that soothing white light surrounding me, but the image kept slipping away.

"You," he spat when he drew near. "Where's the money?"

I glanced at Ronan and Kade, and Ronan shook his head, so I remained silent.

"Bitch," he snarled. "I asked, where's the money?"

"Shut up." Kade's voice was low and dark. "You don't get to talk to her. As far as you're concerned, she doesn't exist. Got it?"

"But she's right there," Parrish pointed out.

I wisely kept my mouth shut.

"Rich and John will get their hands on her sometime," he said, speaking to Kade now. "And it won't be pretty."

Kade twitched, as though he wanted to lunge at Parrish, but Ronan laid a hand on his shoulder to stop him. Parrish sunk onto the chair opposite them.

"Tell us about the riot," Ronan said, his tone even. "Who planned it?"

Parrish gave an insolent shrug. "Don't know. Not my business."

Ronan leaned forward and, for once, I caught a glimpse of the dangerous man beneath the suit. He'd always struck me as a nice guy, but there was nothing nice about the way he stared down Parrish.

"I think it was you," Ronan told him. "You and Rich and John. I think you planned the riot so you'd be able to escape, but you got caught up in the thick of it and they left you behind."

"You don't know anything." But Parrish looked like Ronan had caught him off guard.

"Was it your job to get things started?" Ronan asked. "They made you do the dirty work and then abandoned you?"

Parrish scowled. "It wasn't like that."

Ronan grinned. "Ah, but you did start it?"

"No! I, uh..." He fidgeted. "No."

"They've always been closer to each other than you, haven't they?" The way Ronan stated it like a fact, I almost felt sorry for Parrish. Ronan had clearly struck a nerve and he was going for broke. "Rich and John always look out for each other first. You're just the hired help."

Parrish shot to his feet, and a nearby guard jerked to attention, but then Parrish slowly sat back down. "We look out for each other," he said dully.

"Sure you do." Ronan's tone was dismissive. "What were you planning to do after you were free?"

"Get as far from this shithole as I could," Parrish growled.

"Really?" Kade demanded. "Or were you planning to hunt down Sage and torture her until she told you where the money is?"

Torture?

My stomach rolled, and I sensed both Ronan and Kade turn toward me as if in slow motion.

Who'd said anything about torture?

It made a sick kind of sense. If those men did think I had the money, how else would they make me tell them where it was? But still, something about the factual way Kade had said it made me wonder. Had Jessica been tortured?

Bile rose in the back of my throat and I swallowed—hard—and forced myself to shut down any outward reaction. If I was visibly upset, it might affect how much Parrish was willing to say.

My hearing went fuzzy and I couldn't concentrate on anything as Ronan and Kade continued questioning Parrish. Blood pounded in my ears and I felt myself sway, but I gripped the edges of the seat and held on for dear life. I could get through this, and then I'd demand to know what they'd been keeping from me. Every last detail of it.

13

KADE

Parrish didn't give us any useful information. The entire trip felt like a waste of time. When Ronan had tried to turn Parrish against his friends, it went nowhere. He might be a murderer, but the guy was loyal. And now Sage knew about the torture, or at least suspected. Why couldn't I have kept my big mouth shut? I'd let my fury get the better of me, and now Sage was pale and quiet as we passed back through security.

We stepped onto the sunlit street and her shoulders relaxed slightly, as if being inside the prison had emotionally weighed her down. Perhaps it had. She was a sensitive soul. I didn't believe in mumbo jumbo, but she had a knack for tuning into the mood of a place, and the prison atmosphere had been oppressive.

On the sidewalk, she stopped walking. Ronan and I turned to face her.

"Was Jessica tortured?" she demanded.

I exchanged a glance with Ronan, who nodded. "Yeah."

Tears filled her eyes and her mouth trembled. "How?"

Ronan grimaced. I moved closer to Sage and wrapped an arm around her.

"Do you really want to know?" I asked. "Would it help?"

She sniffled. "I don't know. No, probably not. But I…" She squeezed her eyes shut. "It's all my fault."

"No," I said firmly. "It isn't. It's the fault of the men who tortured her. Their actions are not your responsibility."

"I brought them into her life," she argued.

"They brought themselves into her life," Ronan countered. "They should have been behind bars. You couldn't possibly have known they'd escape, and you shouldn't have to spend your life keeping a distance from everyone just in case someone from your past comes back to haunt you. No one would expect that of you."

I nodded, grateful he'd put my thoughts into words more eloquently than I'd have been able to. "He's right."

"But—"

"No buts." My tone was firm. "None of what happened to her is on you."

She gave a slight nod, but I could tell she didn't agree. For someone who talked about peace and acceptance, she was holding onto a lot of self-blame. I wished I could ease the load.

"Is there anything else you haven't told me?" she asked.

I thought for a moment. "I don't think so. King?"

Ronan shook his head. "Nothing important."

Her forehead scrunched in consternation, but after studying him for a few seconds, she seemed to take his answer at face value. "Okay, then." She dabbed her eyes. "What now?"

Ronan glanced at his watch. "I need to return to the office, so I'll leave you in Kade's capable hands."

Sage hugged Ronan, obviously catching him by surprise. "Tell Willow I love her."

He smiled. "I will."

Ronan walked away, and I mentally ran through our options. We could go back to the cottage, but Sage was emotional and sitting around would do nothing to help that. I couldn't take her anywhere busy because it would be high risk, but surely, we could find some way for her to let off some steam. I shifted, and my holster moved on my hip. An idea slowly took hold.

"Let's go to a shooting range," I suggested. "You keep telling me you're licensed to carry a gun and I want to see what you've got."

Her nose crinkled. "Will that be safe?"

"We'll go to the one I usually use. It's secure and will give us privacy."

She hesitated, then agreed. "Sure, but I might need a refresher."

"No problem." We returned to the car and I drove us to the shooting range, which was housed in a nondescript industrial building on the outskirts of a commercial area. Inside, I asked her to wait while I sorted out bullets and requested the most private space they had. The range wasn't busy, so everything was organized quickly.

Sage looked nervous as we went to the lane furthest away from the others. I loaded my personal handgun, which I preferred to use since it was what I'd rely on in emergencies, and put on my earmuffs, gesturing for her to do the same. She stood back while I lined up the target in my sights and fired twice in quick succession. Both hit dead center.

"Come here," I mouthed, and Sage inched forward. I carefully handed her the gun. She gripped it warily, as though it might bite. I lifted my earmuff and she followed my example so she could hear me better. "Have you used one like this before?"

She eyed it with clear distaste. She may have been able

to shoot, but I got the impression she'd rather not. "Kind of," she said. "But not this exact model."

"Here's how it works." I took it back from her and slowly went through the motions. "Now your turn."

She repeated my actions and aimed at the target, her feet planted a little wider than usual, both hands on the grip. Her long chestnut hair swayed around her hips and my gut wrenched with the urge to bury my face in that sweet-scented mass.

"Good work, but you're not aiming quite right. You won't hit the bullseye like that. Do you mind if I touch you?"

"If you need to." She tensed slightly as I laid a hand on her shoulder, then relaxed. I shifted her arms, guiding her into a better position, trying not to think about the fact I was practically embracing her. Her ass brushed my crotch and I eased back, desperate to keep at least an inch of space between us so she wouldn't know what effect she was having on me. She smelled amazing, and having her so close to me sent all of my senses wild. This was the wrong place to indulge my attraction to her, and it also wouldn't be fair of me to do anything to lead her on when she'd made it clear where we stood. She wanted me to trust her and open up, and I wasn't ready for that. I took a step back, then another.

I cleared my throat. "Earmuffs on, then show me what you've got."

We each covered our ears, A moment later, Sage squeezed the trigger and a shot rang out. The bullet tore a small hole midway between the center and edge of the target.

"Again," I urged.

She adjusted her stance and the next shot hit slightly closer to the center. Her forehead furrowed, making her look adorably focused, and she fired twice more, hitting the target with both, then she lowered the gun and handed it back to me.

"That was really good," I told her. "But we're not done yet. Let's see how you do with your own weapon."

For a moment, I thought she might refuse, but then she nodded, her mouth set in a grim line. "All right."

SAGE

Ever since we'd entered the prison, I'd felt like I was crawling out of my skin. Even hours later, as we drove back into Maple, I couldn't shake the sense of unease. My mind refused to be quiet. Rainforest music didn't help, nor did watching the scenery, or talking things through with Kade. I had a completely illogical sense of impending doom.

I glanced at Kade, wondering about his own mood. He'd been quiet during the drive, but that wasn't unusual. His face was impassive, giving nothing away. When I closed my eyes and tried to probe his aura, I seemed to bounce off him as though he was emitting a forcefield intended to repel me. Maybe he was. I knew he must have felt the sparks flying between us earlier, but he hadn't reacted, and perhaps he'd prefer me to ignore them as well. Acknowledging the attraction would only complicate his job, after all. He needed to be focused, not distracted by me, no matter how much I might have liked him to be.

When we pulled up outside the cottage, I noticed that Sean had left and Vic was leaning against the fence by the side of the house. He seemed to be on his phone, but his eyes were constantly tracking his surroundings, hypervigilant. He was a big guy. Tall and muscular—although not in a way that would make me think he used steroids—with sandy brown hair and sharp green eyes. He nodded as we approached, his gaze skimming over me quickly before landing on Kade.

"Everything good here?" Kade asked.

"Yes, sir. Sean reported that a couple of vehicles went past but they both belonged to people who live nearby. Other than that, it's been quiet. I haven't seen anyone since I arrived."

"Great. You eaten?"

Vic nodded. "I picked up some groceries on the way too."

"Thanks."

We passed Vic, and Kade unlocked the back door to let us in, indicating for me to wait at the entrance while he checked each room. I rolled my eyes. Considering the fact someone had been watching the place constantly since we'd left, it seemed like overkill, but I guessed it was better to be too tight with security than too lax.

Once he'd said it was safe to enter, I prepared a dinner of vegetables and quinoa, hoping the act of cooking would soothe me, but all it did was give me time to dwell on the fact my instincts were telling me something was wrong. When I presented the meal, Kade seemed skeptical, but he ate it anyway. He insisted on cleaning up since I'd done the cooking, so I retreated to the small bedroom I'd claimed and recorded a short mind-clearing meditation for my subscribers. It wasn't enough to empty my own mind of worries, but hopefully it would help someone else.

Then I lounged on the couch, editing the recording on my phone, while Kade sat in the armchair working on his laptop. I still couldn't tell what was going on in his head, and I peeked out at him from beneath my lashes whenever I got the chance. He had such a grounded presence. So strong and steady.

"I'm glad you're here," I told him.

He glanced up, surprised. "Uh, thanks."

"Seriously." I held his gaze. "I know I didn't love the idea of having a bodyguard, and you'd better stay safe or I'll be so mad, but I'm glad it's you who's with me."

His expression softened into a smile. "I am too."

Butterflies took up residence in my stomach. I offered him a tremulous smile, and he returned it. His smile blew me away. It was slightly crooked but made me feel warm inside. It stayed with me even as I slipped into bed later that night.

Perhaps that was the reason I didn't notice anything wrong until it was almost too late.

14

———

SAGE

I drifted in and out of sleep. I was restless, tossing and turning, unable to get comfortable, and that creeping sensation of dread followed me into my dreams.

I dreamed I was eighteen and back in my bedroom, listening to my parents fight. Except this time, I didn't ignore them. I tiptoed down the hall and into the living room just in time to see Dad shove Mom, and Mom trip over a cord and fall. Her head smacked the tiled hearth and blood exploded everywhere—far too much blood to be realistic. I screamed and tore at my face, trying to get it off my skin and the taste out of my mouth.

Suddenly, other men were in the room. Faces I'd seen too much of in courtrooms and in the news. Baker, with his cruel blue eyes. Getty, who radiated menace despite his short stature. Parrish, as bitter as he'd been in prison. A brief flash of LaMond. Their faces seemed to close in on me, taunting me. I ran from the room, but it felt like my feet were moving through molasses. The harder I tried to run, the slower I went.

Then I was outside. Dad was behind me, yelling at me to

save myself. I threw myself at the fence, but there were no broken pieces for me to use as footholds. A pair of hands grabbed me and hauled me to the ground, then circled around my throat and squeezed. I looked up and saw Dad staring back at me, his features twisted with hate. I tried to speak. To tell him I didn't understand. But his face morphed. Grew darker and less distinct.

I blinked, my mind whirring helplessly as the world around me seemed to spin and refocus.

I was in a dark room.

A man knelt over me, his hands around my throat.

I couldn't breathe.

I tried to haul in a lungful of air and my eyes prickled. I couldn't *breathe*. And I wasn't dreaming. This man was really here, kneeling above me, choking the life out of me. I couldn't even yell for help.

I bucked, struggling to throw him off, and it bought me enough space to suck in a little air. Enough to keep fighting. I rammed up with my knee and threw my weight to the side. We tumbled off the edge of the bed and his back thumped the wall on the way down.

He smacked me across the face and I cried out, the taste of blood reminding me of that awful dream. He grabbed my shoulders and slammed me against the floor. The edges of my vision grew hazy but I lashed out. I wasn't going to make this easy for him. At the very least, Kade should have heard us by now.

He grabbed for my throat again and I plunged two fingers into his face, feeling one hit something soft. He grunted, and then the bedroom door was torn open.

KADE

Terror and fury clawed at my insides as I tried to make sense of what I was seeing. Sage was on the floor, struggling against a man in a balaclava.

I rushed in and, with a few swift, economical movements, tore the assailant off her and threw him to the ground. I heard a shout, and then I was on him. I pounded a fist into his masked face. Then another. My mind seemed to fog out and I was operating on autopilot, pummeling the guy, unable to rid myself of the image of Sage fighting for her life. I'd never been more scared. But she was okay. Thank God.

My limbs kept moving of their own accord. Hitting with devastating force. He deserved it, this man who'd tried to hurt my wild child.

"Kade."

A soft voice infiltrated my thoughts, breaking through the haze that had overwhelmed me.

"Kade, look at me."

I wanted to, but animal instinct was driving me to make sure the intruder no longer posed a threat.

"Sweetheart, stop."

I stopped. My hands fell to my sides, and as the fog retreated further, my knuckles began to throb.

"You're okay." A soothing hand rubbed my upper back. "Shh," Sage murmured. "It's okay. I'm safe, you're safe, and he's not going anywhere."

"Get the light." My tone was dull. Despair had started creeping over me. I'd saved Sage, but she'd seen the monster that lived inside of me. She'd seen what I was capable of, and she couldn't possibly want anything to do with me now.

She flicked a switch and harsh white light illuminated the room, making the scene around me seem even more horrific. My hands were speckled with blood, and I could feel flecks of it on my face and chest. I'd come running straight from bed, so I was only wearing boxers. The man on the floor was a mess. I nudged him, and he groaned. Relief filled me. I couldn't imagine how much emotional damage it would have caused if I'd beaten him to death in front of Sage.

"Fuck," I muttered. "Call an ambulance."

"I already have." She held up a phone. "Just hold on and I'll give them the address."

I stared at the multicolored shadows forming around her throat and my stomach lurched sickeningly. "You... He... Fuck, baby. Come here." I got shakily to my feet and pulled her closer so I could look at it. "I'm so sorry." I felt like kicking the prone man for what he'd done to her. "I should have protected you."

Her eyebrows knitted together. "You saved me. I knew if I could just hold him off for long enough, you'd come, and you did."

"But..." I glanced down at my knuckles, the spots of red contrasting against my skin like dozens of tiny accusations. I hated that she'd seen me like that. God, what must she think of me? I shook myself. "We need to call Ronan."

She nodded. "I'll do it while you check on him." She gestured to the intruder.

"I'm on it." While she returned her attention to her phone, I patted the intruder down and removed a gun and a knife. Jesus, he'd come prepared. Suddenly, I went cold. Where was Vic? I glanced at Sage, but she was still talking. When she finished, I nodded toward the door. "Vic."

The color leached out of Sage's cheeks, and she started toward the exit.

"No, wait." I couldn't let her go outside alone. "We'll go find him together, in a minute. Can you go into my bedroom and get the handcuffs from the bedside table?" She nodded and hurried out. I reached for the bottom of the guy's balaclava and peeled it up, wincing as I realized it was soaked with blood. My doing. I probed his face to see where the blood was coming from, but it seemed to be his nose and lip, neither of which meant anything serious. When he spat a curse word and tried to sit up, I felt weirdly relieved.

Sage reappeared, holding out a pair of metal handcuffs. I cuffed the guy to a cabinet. Under normal circumstances, he'd be able to get away reasonably easily, but I didn't think he was going anywhere. Still, I didn't want to leave him.

"On second thought," I said. "You stay here." I reached for her purse and emptied it, pulling out the spare gun I'd given her that she still kept inside. "Aim this at his torso and shoot if he so much as moves."

"Okay," she whispered, a torn look in her eyes that said she didn't want to shoot him but was prepared to if it came down to it. My little pacifist had a core of steel. A wave of affection slammed into me and I dropped a kiss on her cheek, surprised when she didn't flinch away. She'd seen how I turned that guy into pulp with my bare hands. How was she not afraid of me?

I took the intruder's gun, musing on the fact he hadn't tried to use it—what was that about?—and moved silently through the cottage room by room. I didn't want to leave until I was sure nobody was hiding in a closet and planning to attack as soon as I was gone. Once I was certain Sage was secure in the house with the intruder, I headed outside. It took only a couple of minutes to find Vic slumped against the wall, bleeding from an injury to the back of his head. I gave his shoulder a gentle shake.

"Vic," I hissed.

He murmured something incomprehensible, then jolted and sat upright, wincing as his head injury made itself known. "Wha' happened?"

I stood, gripped his arm, and hauled him up. It would be

best if we got inside. Out here we'd be sitting ducks. "My best guess is you were struck from behind."

I ushered him inside, keeping an arm around him until we reached Sage's bedroom. His eyes widened slightly at the sight of the guy on the floor, but then he lowered himself onto the bed and touched a finger to the back of his head.

"Sorry." He looked mortified. "I let you down. I can't believe he got the drop on me."

"He'd probably been watching you, waiting for the right moment," I said, trying to think clearly. "He must have tracked us while we were in the city and followed us out here, staying far enough back to be out of sight."

"I should have noticed him," Vic grumbled.

"So should I." I'd been off my game, distracted by Sage, and it had nearly gotten her killed—if that had been the intruder's intention.

"Can I get a first aid kit?" Sage asked. "Or do you need me to stay here?"

"Go, but take a gun."

She pressed her lips into a grim line but did as I said. When she reentered, she opened the first aid kit on the bed and approached Vic. "I'm going to use an antiseptic wipe on your injury. Is that okay?"

"Yeah," he grunted. "I don't think it's bad. I've just got a hell of a headache."

He gritted his teeth while she wiped his wound clean and handed him a clean white cloth to press to it if it started bleeding.

"Let me check you too," she said, coming over to me.

"The blood isn't mine," I protested.

Her eyes narrowed. "Humor me."

I studied her face for a moment, wondering what she saw when she looked at me, but then nodded my consent. She grabbed another antiseptic wipe and gently cleaned my face. The tenderness was such a contrast to the brutality of the past ten minutes that emotion burned at the back of my throat.

"Aren't you scared of me?" I asked, loud enough that only she could hear.

"No." Her eyes searched mine. "I'm sorry that you had to be violent on my behalf, but I'm not afraid of you." She leaned forward and pressed a chaste kiss to my cheek. "You're a good man."

I clenched my fists and battled to keep my emotions in check. "You're too good for this world."

"No. But it's nice that you see me that way." She shifted away again and knelt beside the intruder, who'd opened his eyes and was watching us in sullen silence. "The paramedics should be here soon," she told him. "I'm just going to clean you up, if you'll let me."

I shook my head, amazed. How could she be kind even to the man who'd been strangling her? She was incredible. I certainly didn't deserve her admiration, but deep down, I had to admit, I liked it. Maybe a little too much.

15

———

KADE

The ambulance arrived first. Thankfully, by the time the paramedics had assisted the intruder into the ambulance, keeping him handcuffed even though they were clearly skeptical as to whether it was necessary, a pair of police constables had also arrived and arranged with one of the paramedics to accompany him to the hospital. I sat with Sage and Vic while another paramedic checked Vic's head wound.

"It'll hurt for a while, but you don't need stitches," the paramedic told him. "It doesn't look like you have a concussion, but you should take the rest of your shift off and make sure you have someone around to monitor you just in case."

Vic glanced at me, and I nodded to show I agreed.

"One of the others can drive you back into town later," I said. "Just to be safe."

"Thanks." He sighed. I knew he still felt guilty that the intruder had gotten past him.

"Don't beat yourself up," I added. "It's happened to us all at some point."

I meant it, but I was also relieved that I'd been here so

Vic's slipup hadn't been deadly. If I'd left Sage to the care of my team as I would another client, would she be gone now?

Vic scowled. "That doesn't mean I have to like it."

The paramedic shifted from him to Sage. "Tilt your head so I can see your throat better," she said, supporting Sage's head with one of her hands while she angled it back. She scanned the bruises, which were definitely finger-shaped. The sight of them marring her otherwise flawless skin made me want to drag the asshole back here and throttle him to see how he liked it. "Does it hurt to speak?"

"Only a little," Sage said. Her voice was huskier than usual. A vein throbbed at my temple in response. Vic and I had both let her down. Our sole job right now was to protect her, and we'd failed.

No, *I'd* failed. At the end of the day, I knew her safety came down to me. I couldn't blame anyone else for failing her.

The paramedic checked her pupil reflexes. "Are you hurt anywhere else?"

"No. I had a fright, but I don't think he actually did much damage."

"Good." The paramedic stepped back and smiled sympathetically. "The same goes for you as for Vic. Take it easy and stay near someone in case it turns out you have an injury that isn't immediately obvious."

Sage nodded. "Thanks."

The paramedic turned to me, but I shook my head. "I'm fine."

My knuckles ached, but I wasn't about to mention that, and even if I did, it wasn't as though they could do anything about it.

"Okay, then. It seems my job here is done." The paramedic's expression became stern. "No more excitement from you people."

"Yes, ma'am," Vic said with a teasing salute.

She rolled her eyes on the way out the door.

I was about to ask Sage whether she really was okay but before I got the chance, Joanna walked in with Ronan and Willow close behind. Willow flew across the room and gathered Sage into her arms. They spoke in hushed voices and clutched at each other. I tried to focus on the others, not wanting to intrude on their private conversation.

"How do you think they found you?" Ronan asked under his breath.

"I'd say they staked out the prison and followed us from there," I muttered. "They must have realized we'd question Parrish."

"If you didn't see anyone following you, they were good," he said.

"I know." It made me nervous. The guy who'd broken into the cottage hadn't been either Getty or Baker, so I had to wonder if they'd hired a professional.

Ronan sighed. "You can't stay here."

"I know, but it'll take a few hours to organize something else." I glanced at Sage again. "In the meantime, I'm going to position extra guards outside."

He nodded. "Several of your men are already on their way."

"Thanks, King."

"Was he trying to abduct her?" Joanna asked quietly.

My stomach cramped. "I don't know. He had his hands around her throat. He might have been trying to kill her."

She frowned. "But she's no use to them dead."

I shrugged. "I'm just telling you what I saw, Jo. I don't know what he was planning. Hopefully he'll talk when you question him."

"Mm." Her lips were pinched. "We'll see."

Sage and Willow broke apart.

Joanna blanked her expression and cleared her throat loudly enough to get everyone's attention. "I'll need to take statements from Kade, Sage, and Vic," she said. "We'll do that in the kitchen. I've also brought a photographer who will need to gather photographic evidence of any injuries. Is everyone okay with that?"

We all agreed.

"Great, I'll start with Sage." She gestured for Sage to follow her out of the room. My stomach plummeted as Sage left my sight. Logically, I knew she'd be safe with Joanna, but my heart didn't want to risk leaving her unguarded. I could still recall the terror I'd felt at seeing her fighting for her life. It was too fresh.

The police's questioning and evidence collection took several hours. By the time everyone other than Sage, me, and a few guards departed, the dark sky was beginning to lighten into dawn. I was weary, but adrenaline kept me going. Sage must have been bone tired. She was quiet and withdrawn and had been for some time.

"Would you like to get out of here?" I asked.

She frowned. "The new safe house isn't ready yet, is it?"

"No, but we could go to the office." I'd suggest a hotel room, but there were too many variables. We wouldn't be able to make it secure. At least here we now had several layers of security in place.

"This is fine." She sighed. "Honestly, I need a nap. Do you mind if I use your bed?"

The police had taken the bedclothes from her bed as evidence.

"No problem." I hesitated, then added, "Do you want me in there with you?" I hated the thought of leaving her vulnerable again.

"I'd like that, thanks. You may as well get a nap too."

I'd been about to stand, but I stopped, taken aback. "I don't mind dragging a chair in there."

She offered a small smile. "Don't be silly. The bed is big enough for both of us. Besides, I like the idea of having you close."

Okay, then. I wasn't about to argue just for the sake of it. Sage went to the bedroom and I updated the guys outside. When I returned, I cleaned up in the bathroom and went to join her. Sage was beneath the covers, curled on her side. I considered taking my shirt and pants off but decided I'd better not. I didn't want to make her uncomfortable. I closed the door and got into the bed fully clothed, lying as far away from her as I could.

For a few minutes, the only sound in the room was our breathing, but then there was a rustle as she moved. I felt her slip closer to me, her back pressing against my side.

I smiled slowly and rose up on an elbow. "If you want snuggles, that's all you have to say."

Her cheeks turned pink. "I need snuggles."

"You've come to the right place." I rolled onto my side and wrapped my arm around her waist so her back flattened against my chest. "Better?"

She released a contented sigh. "Yes, thanks. I feel so much safer when you're holding me."

I nearly scoffed. I had no idea how she could feel that way when she'd seen the violence I was capable of.

"What is it?" she asked quietly. "You're stressed about something."

My jaw tensed. "It's just that I don't get how you can be so relaxed with me when you saw what I did to that guy earlier."

She snuggled closer. "Like I said, you're a good person. I know that in my heart."

"But how can you?" I protested, unreasonably annoyed by her attitude. "You don't know what I've done in the past."

She placed her hands over mine and stroked rhythmic circles on my skin. "So, tell me."

"What if you can't stand the sight of me afterward?" I didn't know how I'd handle that.

"Then I'll stay right here, in your arms, with my eyes shut, and it won't be a problem because I won't be able to see you anyway."

"Don't be flippant," I snapped.

"I'm not." She was frustratingly calm despite my outburst. "No matter what I say, it won't ease your mind, but it seems like you need to unburden yourself, and I'm here to listen. It's up to you what, or how much, you want to share."

I mulled over her words, still holding her close, as though she might slip away if I loosened my grip. "Okay." *Here goes.* "You remember how I told you that I did one year of college and then joined the military?"

"Yes."

"Well, the military wasn't exactly my choice." I waited to feel her tense or for her to roll over so we were facing each other, but she stayed put, perhaps sensing that was what I needed. "I made a mistake, and that was the best option left to me."

"What mistake did you make?" Her voice was quiet. Accepting. We'd see how long that lasted.

"One of my college friends was a girl called Charlotte. She was a friendly, outgoing person, but in the second semester of our first year, something changed. She seemed sad all the time. I asked her what was wrong, but she just brushed me off. I was worried about her, so a friend and I decided to check in each day to make sure she was all right. One day, I visited her dorm room and..." My lungs grew tight. I tried to haul in air. In my arms, Sage wriggled around until I could see the concern in her warm brown eyes. She kissed my cheek but didn't say anything, and finally, I was able to continue. "She was just lying there, on the bed." My voice cracked. "She'd overdosed on prescription meds."

"Oh, Kade. I'm so sorry."

I tucked her head beneath my chin and cradled her against my body, greedy for the comfort she provided. "They reckoned she'd been there for a couple of days. My friend was supposed to have been checking on her that week, but he'd been distracted with a new girlfriend and had forgotten. It was awful."

I'd never get the image out of my head. At first, I'd thought my eyes were deceiving me, but then the horrible truth had sunk in.

"She left a letter," I continued, my voice hoarse. "It explained that she'd been raped by another student. He was from a filthy rich family. When she told him she'd go to the police, he said no one would believe her. He'd really gotten inside her head. She couldn't live with what had happened and truly thought that nobody would be on her side." I gritted my teeth, my jaw painfully stiff. "I was furious. With her, for not realizing that I would have believed her. With my friend, for not being there like he was supposed to. But most of all, with the monster who thought he'd gotten away with it."

Sage pressed a chaste kiss to my chest, and it sent a flicker of warmth through me, disrupting the despair and grief that descended whenever I thought of Charlotte.

"I found the guy who did it and beat the crap out of him," I confessed. "It was like something took over my body and I couldn't stop. All of this pain and anger just exploded out of me and I took it all out on him."

When I temporarily fell silent, Sage prompted me. "What happened next?"

I bit my lip while I got my emotions under control. No matter how many years had passed, I'd never forget how I felt that day. "I made it very clear to my friend what I thought of him for being careless with Charlotte's wellbeing. We haven't talked since. The raping asshole didn't press charges because that would mean the contents of Charlotte's suicide letter might come out in court."

"That's good, right?"

"There are other ways to punish someone. His family were powerful and they threatened to wreck me unless I joined the military and left the country. They didn't want me anywhere near their precious boy. My parents and Audrey were vulnerable, so I went along with it. In the end, it worked out well. The army suited me. But I hate that they were able to destroy a sweet girl who'd done nothing wrong and then bully me into submission without any consequences." I'd loathed that I hadn't been able to get that monster arrested for the rape since there had been no evidence remaining, and that I'd lost control of myself when I tracked him down. The entire situation had been sickening.

"So, this man is still out there?" Sage asked.

"No," I said darkly. "When Ronan and I were in a position to do it, we found evidence that he'd assaulted other girls and worked behind the scenes with our contacts in the legal profession to help them build a case and have him convicted. He's in prison, where he belongs."

SAGE

I drew back so I could see Kade's face. His dark eyes were awash with emotion, and I could tell he expected me to withdraw from him. He clearly held himself at least partially responsible for what had happened with Charlotte and for the ugliness of the aftermath. In a way, I understood much better now where his tendency to hold himself responsible for everything came from, and why he'd stepped in after we saw Getty outside that coffee shop what felt like weeks ago now. He didn't trust anyone else to do what needed to be done. His friend had let him down in the past, and then Kade hadn't reacted the way he thought he should have. This must be why he didn't consider himself worthy of me.

I considered my next words carefully. He was poised to push me away and I didn't want to give him any excuse to. "It must have been difficult for you. You were only young— your friend too—and I doubt either of you had any experience in dealing with that kind of thing."

Kade grunted something that could have been agreement. "But he still should have checked on her. Hell, *I* should have checked on her. I shouldn't have just given up any of the responsibility for making sure she was okay. I knew what my friend was like when he met a new girl, and I still let it happen."

"Her death was tragic," I said. "But it wasn't your fault. She must have felt like she was backed into a corner. People make terrible mistakes when they think they have no way out."

"I should have been there for her." He sounded anguished. "I should have made her tell me what had happened."

The years obviously hadn't healed this emotional wound. Instead, it had festered.

"You couldn't force her to do that," I replied. "You did what you thought best at the time. It's easy to see what could have been done differently in hindsight, but when you're neck-deep in a situation, nothing is quite so clear."

"I knew she was unhappy."

"And you asked about it, but she didn't want to talk," I pointed out. "You agreed to a buddy system with your friend. You did the best you could."

His face twisted into an ugly sneer. "I offloaded responsibility to someone I should have known wouldn't be up to the job, and then I beat a guy until he was nearly unrecognizable. I don't think that's doing 'my best.'"

I rested a hand over his heart. It was thudding hard and fast. "You're good in here."

"How do you know that?" His expression changed to something pleading, as if he actually wanted me to convince him of his own inherent decency. "I thought I'd changed, but I didn't need to punch that guy who broke in here. Once I'd subdued him, I should have stopped. But I didn't, because I haven't changed at all. I'm violent, and maybe you should be scared of me. I don't trust anyone—not even myself—and you shouldn't either."

My heart hurt because I could tell he actually believed what he was saying. "You've given me no reason to be scared of you or to doubt you."

He stared at me in disbelief. "Haven't you been listening?"

"Yes." I rubbed my palm over his beating heart. "What I hear is that you're a man who lost a friend and did some things he isn't proud of. But you're not the devil you make yourself out to be, and you don't have a monopoly on self-blame."

He frowned. "What do you mean?"

I bit my lip. If I wanted him to really hear me, I needed to share something important, the way he'd done with me. "I'm either directly or indirectly responsible for four deaths. Most of the time, I manage not to blame myself, but sometimes I can't help it. Just like you, I can't stop the 'what ifs.'

What if I'd interrupted Mom and Dad's argument—would Mom still be alive? What if I hadn't been so determined to go to the dramatic arts college—would Dad never have decided to help rob a bank? If I hadn't been born, would he have had a life of crime at all, or had he only done that to try to provide for me?"

I blew out a soft breath and gathered myself before continuing. "If I'd been better at defending myself, would Craig have died to save me, or would I not have needed him to do that? If I'd decided not to get a roommate, would Jessica be painting in an attic somewhere else in Chicago at this very minute?" I let everything I was feeling shine in my eyes. "There are so many 'what ifs,' I could drown in them. But what if, painful though it might be, everything happened the way it was supposed to?"

He shook his head. "How am I meant to believe that when horrible things happen to good people?"

"I don't know," I whispered. "But you have to believe in something or you'll never be able to move on with your life."

He touched soft lips to my forehead. "I believe in you."

I smiled. "That's a start."

"I believe that keeping you safe is more important than anything else," he murmured.

My stomach swooped and dipped. "That's sweet, but keeping yourself safe is also important. Please be careful. I know I said I try to believe things happen for a reason, but I don't want you dying for me. You deserve better than that."

He traced the outline of my cheek with his thumb, then followed with his lips, trailing kisses from my forehead to my mouth.

"You deserve everything," he said, and then he kissed me.

16

KADE

Sage tasted of mint and chamomile from the tea she'd drunk before we went to bed. I ended the kiss and released a slow breath, mesmerized by the imprint of her lips against mine.

"Everything," I repeated, needing her to know how much she meant to me. She was incredible, my wild child, and I still didn't think I deserved her, but damned if I could continue resisting. I'd nearly lost her, and it had helped me see that I couldn't be without her. Not ever again.

To my surprise, she closed the distance between us and brushed her lips over mine. Where I'd pulled back after only a couple of seconds, she pressed closer and deepened the kiss. I placed a hand on her curvy hip to steady her. When her tongue stroked mine, I groaned, but resisted the urge to rub my hardening cock against her. She needed to rest. Now wasn't the time for that.

But then she cupped her hand around my erection and wedged one of her legs between mine. And hell, maybe now was the time for that. After all, we weren't guaranteed tomorrow.

"Is this okay?" she asked. Her free hand caressed the side of my neck and rubbed across my trimmed beard.

"Very," I murmured, holding her gaze as I slipped the hand that had been on her hip beneath the hem of her pajama pants and down the satiny skin of her thigh. She arched into my touch like a cat, and her breath hitched. She was so sensitive.

"Are you sure about this?" I had to ask. It had been a stressful day, and I didn't want her to regret anything later.

But she smiled that beautiful, peaceful smile I loved so much. "I am."

"Good." I peppered kisses up the length of her neck, so softly that my lips barely scraped her skin. She sighed and pressed closer, her hands slipping behind me to explore the planes of my back beneath my t-shirt. She shimmied her pajama bottoms off and I felt the heat of her sex against my leg. I grabbed her shapely ass and shifted her so that she was effectively straddling my thigh, her underwear the only barrier between us. She whimpered and ground herself against me.

"Yes, baby, just like that," I urged. "I want to make you feel good."

"You do." Her eyelashes fluttered open. "You make me feel good just by existing."

"Jesus, what did I do to deserve you?" I claimed her mouth, my cock hard as hell within the confines of my sweatpants, but I didn't want to let her go for long enough to take them off.

Her hips rocked and she let out a husky moan. I worked my hand inside her panties and slipped a finger between her folds. She was slick and gasped as I stroked her, then drew ever-tightening circles around her clit. She shuddered in my arms, and I pushed one of my fingers inside her and crooked it.

"Oh, God," she cried.

"Quiet, love." I kissed her forehead. "We don't want the guards outside to think something is happening to you."

I moved my finger inside her tight channel. She narrowed her eyes, then pulled away and shoved my sweatpants down. I threw the blankets out of the way but then gripped the sheets as she removed my underwear and wrapped a hand around my cock. She gave me a teasing smile, then stripped off her top and panties, crawled down the bed and licked the throbbing head.

Fuck.

I sucked in a shallow breath and tried to stay calm, but then she wrapped her velvety mouth around me and all rational thought fled. I fisted the sheets to keep from grabbing her head and shoving my cock deeper into her mouth. She licked up the length, holding my gaze, and it was the sexiest fucking thing I'd ever seen. She teased me with gentle kisses until I was a panting mess and couldn't take any more of it.

I flipped her beneath me and wriggled down until I set my mouth over her pussy and got to work, determined to drive her as crazy as she'd made me. She gasped, then clapped a hand to her mouth as I licked and sucked and stroked her. When I felt her hips buck and tension override her body, I eased back and searched for a condom in the toiletries bag on the nightstand.

"I want to make love to you," I told her, so there couldn't be any confusion. This wasn't just sex. It meant something.

"I want that more than anything." She took the condom from me and rolled it down my cock. When it was on, she lay back and spread her legs.

"Fuck." I took in the sight of her, with flushed cheeks and beard burn on her thighs. She looked exquisite. She looked *mine*. "You're stunning."

I sunk into her slowly, savoring the delicious sensation. She intertwined her legs with mine and kissed me, making soft sounds into my mouth as I drew back and pumped into her again. My heart squeezed. I'd never felt so at one with another person. Our tongues tangled in a drugging kiss, and I made love to her in slow rhythmic thrusts, adoring the way she came apart beneath me.

I ran my hands over every beautiful bit of her, wishing I could make this last forever. I'd wanted her for so long and she felt so good. I toyed with one of her nipples and buried my face in the crook of her neck, sucking the tender skin there as I moved inside her.

"Oh!" Her eyes flew open and locked on mine as she came. The combination of emotion and pleasure I saw in them pushed me over the brink and I growled her name as I pulsed into the condom. A shudder tore through me, and I propped myself on my arms, careful not to flatten her.

We stayed in that position until our breathing had leveled out and our hearts had returned to their usual speed, then I kissed her forehead and rolled off. I disposed of the condom and lay beside her again, pulling her into my arms. She felt so right there. I never wanted to let her go. I was halfway in love with Sage, and I'd never felt quite so vulnerable. She'd seen all the ugly parts of me and hadn't run away. Did I dare hope she could one day love me too?

SAGE

We dozed in a post-sex haze until the shrill ring of Kade's phone woke us. He grunted and flopped his arm out of bed, reaching for the phone on the nightstand.

"Campbell," he answered gruffly.

Whatever the person at the other end said, it made him

sit up and open his eyes, so I did the same, watching his face for any indication of what the conversation might be about.

"Already?" he asked and glanced at his watch. "Has the guy from this morning been questioned yet?" There was a pause as he listened intently. "Uh-huh." He nodded. "Thanks. We'll be there soon." He ended the call.

"Who was that?" I asked.

"Zeke." His face did that weird twitchy thing it seemed to do when he mentioned Zeke. "The new safe house is ready to go. It's in an apartment building not far from King's place."

"That's good," I said. "Right?"

I, for one, was eager to get out of this cottage. In hindsight, I was amazed I'd been able to relax here for long enough to make love with Kade. I supposed the intensity of our emotions had made it impossible to think of anything else.

"Yeah." He rolled out of bed and gathered his clothes. "The police have interviewed the man who broke in, and they're allowing King to have a word with him shortly. I'd like to observe."

"Can I be there too?"

"Behind the observation mirror." He gave me a warning look. "You're not getting into the same room as that scumbag."

I shrugged. "Fine with me."

Kade's eyes tracked downward and I flushed. I'd forgotten I was naked. I didn't cover myself though. I wasn't ashamed of my body, and he seemed to like what he saw. I slid my feet off the edge of the bed and pulled my pajamas back on. I'd have to get other clothes from my own bedroom. I only hoped none of the guards outside had heard us earlier. I waited until Kade was decent, then opened the door and crossed the hall. My new clothes were piled in the corner of the room—presumably an officer had rifled through them to check for evidence—and I put on a pair of pale blue yoga pants and a white top. There was a roaring sound overhead, and I frowned. What could possibly be making that much noise?

"Sage?" Kade appeared in the doorway. "Are you packed?"

"I can be in a couple of minutes." I gestured toward the ceiling. "What's that?"

"King sent a chopper to take us to the police station so we don't miss the interrogation."

My eyebrows flew up. I hated to think how much all of this must be costing Ronan.

"It's not a big deal," he said, apparently reading my expression. "The company owns the chopper and the pilot works for us. Grab your things."

I shoved the clothes into a bag and packed my toiletries. "What about the food?"

"The guards will take it home. Don't worry, it won't go to waste. You ready?"

I nodded, and he took my hand and led me outside. The chopper had landed in the center of the street, dull gray in the morning light. I noticed that several of the neighbors were staring in fascination through their windows. It was just as well we weren't trying to be discreet anymore because this would have the entire neighborhood gossiping. Kade escorted me to the chopper and I climbed up inside, taking one of the seats behind the pilot. Kade sat beside me and the pilot shut the door and donned a headset. A few minutes later, we were hovering over Chicago. I gazed over the cityscape, trying to see as much of it as I could. I'd never been in a helicopter before, and the view was much better than it was through the tiny windows of a plane. I picked out a few key buildings against the skyline. The Willis Tower. The St Regis.

We slowly descended, landing atop a blocky brick building. Kade and I stayed seated until the pilot opened the hatch and waved us off. A pair of uniformed officers stood near the landing pad, awaiting our arrival.

"The interview is about to begin," one of them called over the whirring of the blades. "Come this way."

They led us through a dingy building with off-white walls and wooden frames around the windows and doors. We went down two flights of stairs and entered a corridor, off which we were guided into a small chamber with a portal that looked into another room, where Ronan was seated opposite a lean man with a bruised face and a swollen eye socket. I studied the man, wondering if I might recognize him from the past. He could be one of Dad's former acquaintances. But he didn't look familiar. The door in the other room opened and Ronan glanced over. He gave a slight nod to whoever was at the entrance, then cleared his throat. I was surprised by how well the sound carried through.

"Can they see us?" I asked the officer who'd remained with us.

"No. The window looks like a mirror from their side," he replied.

"How much did he tell Detective Lee?" Kade asked.

The officer gave him a reproachful look. "I can't say."

"Fair enough."

I sunk onto an uncomfortable plastic chair and settled in to watch.

"Peter Black," Ronan said, placing a closed manila folder on the table in front of himself. "You have quite a record. Dishonorably discharged from the navy. Two counts of assault, one of breaking and entering, and a D.U.I. Do you prefer to be called 'Peter' or 'Mr. Black'?"

Peter Black's shoulders were slumped, but he raised his eyes from the tabletop temporarily. "Don't care."

"Then we'll go with 'Peter.'" Ronan's tone was brisk but almost friendly. "Let's get to the point, Peter. Why did you break into the cottage in Maple and attempt to strangle Miss Nichols in the early hours of this morning?"

Peter sighed. "I wasn't trying to kill her. I just needed to knock her out so I could get her into the car, and that seemed like the quietest way to do it."

It was strange, how cavalierly he spoke of abducting me. I couldn't fathom a lifestyle where that wasn't something out of the ordinary.

"Why?" Ronan repeated.

Peter shrugged one shoulder, then winced in pain. "A couple of guys paid me to do it. I was supposed to drop her at a rest stop off the highway between Chicago and Maple."

Ronan opened the folder and slid a photograph across the table. I couldn't see the details of the image, but when Peter nodded and said, "Yeah, that's them," I assumed it must be a picture of Getty and Baker.

"The police have already checked at the rest stop," the officer beside me murmured. "They weren't there. When Black didn't turn up on time, they must have realized something was wrong."

"Damn," Kade muttered.

"How well do you know Richard Getty and Johnathan Baker?" Ronan asked.

"I don't." Peter sounded defeated. "I just had the shitty luck of meeting them at a bar and overhearing them say they needed someone for a job. I'm broke so I volunteered."

"Did you realize they were escaped convicts?"

"Nah. I don't watch much TV."

"Did they tell you why they wanted someone else to do the abduction rather than going after her themselves?"

"I just figured they didn't want to get their hands dirty. You know how some guys are. Don't care how it happens as long as they don't have to do it themselves." His expression turned wry. "I'm starting to think they knew she'd be protected and didn't want to risk their own asses."

"Maybe," Ronan agreed. "Did they say anything else?"

Peter scowled. "I'm just the hired help, what do you think?"

The air shifted beside me and then I felt the heat of Kade's palm on my lower back. Warmth radiated through me at his silent show of support. I'd spent so much time with only Willow to rely on, it was nice to know he was there for me.

"Think carefully," Ronan said.

Peter rolled his eyes. "I overheard them saying they needed to visit some old friends."

A prickle crept down the back of my neck. I wondered what that meant. Perhaps they'd decided that one of Dad's buddies might have known what he'd planned and would be able to lead them to the money.

"One last question." Ronan steepled his fingers. "Do you think they'll send someone else after Miss Nichols?"

Peter cocked his head. "Yeah. Whatever they're looking for, they want it bad. That girl is gonna be in danger until they find it."

I shivered, suddenly feeling very exposed. Kade's arm tightened around my waist and I leaned into the shelter of his body and let myself soak up his comforting strength. He kissed my temple and tears prickled at the backs of my eyes. I adored this big, protective man. I only hoped I wouldn't get him killed.

17

KADE

As soon as the interview ended, we returned to the chopper, with Ronan accompanying us, and flew to King's Security headquarters. Sage looked pale, and I got the feeling she'd been rattled by what Peter Black said, so I kept her hand firmly in mine while we made our way through the building to Ronan's office.

Each of the directors had a well-appointed office, but Ronan's was undoubtedly the best, with floor-to-ceiling windows and a spectacular view over the city. He had a heavy wooden desk and another table along the wall, which the three of us—plus Zeke, who'd been waiting for our arrival—clustered around.

"Do you need anything?" Fiona, Ronan's personal assistant, asked from the doorway. I flashed her a quick smile. The statuesque redhead was the most efficient woman I'd ever met. I wouldn't mind someone like her to help manage my own schedule, but I hadn't gotten around to hiring anyone yet.

Zeke perked up. "Coffee?"

Fiona narrowed her eyes. "Get your own."

I smirked. For whatever reason, Fiona seemed to be the only woman in the building who didn't fall prey to Zeke's wannabe rock star good looks.

"No, we've got everything we need," Ronan said. "Thank you, Fiona."

Fiona smiled politely and left the room.

"So, what did he say?" Zeke asked, lounging back in his chair with his hands behind his head. For some reason, that irritated me. To be fair, most things Zeke did irritated me, but only because he never seemed to take anything seriously—and on the few occasions when he did, he always used underhanded tactics.

"He was sent to abduct Sage, not kill her," Ronan told him, and filled him in quickly on what else Peter Black had said.

Zeke's dark brows knitted together, his silver eyebrow ring bright against them. "What do you think he meant by 'visiting old friends'?"

"I think they're going to track down my father's friends and interrogate them." To my surprise, it was Sage who'd spoken.

Zeke pursed his lips, studying her with interest. "You might be right," he said thoughtfully. "Perhaps we should do the same."

"What do you mean?" I demanded.

He slung an arm over the top of the chair and turned to me, his expression touched with amusement. "If we want to find them before they take another shot at Sage, then our best bet is to intercept them. Sage, do you know who your father used to spend his time with?"

"A bit." She glanced from me to Zeke and wet her lips. "I met a few of his friends, and I can tell you some of his old hangouts, but I'm sure there's a heap I don't know. It's not like he confided everything in his teenage daughter."

"Whatever you know is likely more than we do," Zeke pointed out. "I think we should follow their example and see what we find."

I glanced at Ronan, certain he'd dismiss the idea, but he seemed to be considering it.

"No," I snapped because someone had to say it. "If we do that, we'll be putting Sage at a higher degree of risk. It would be safer for us to stay under the radar and wait for them to surface."

"Who knows how long that will take?" Zeke sounded exasperated. "They want whatever knowledge they think Sage has. They're out of luck, but there's no reason we can't use what she knows to get a head start."

I glared at him. "You always want to use people. It's not safe, or fair."

A delicate cough interrupted us.

"Actually," Sage said, seeing that she had our attention. "I agree with Zeke." She reached for my hand. "If we can end this sooner, it means there's less chance of anyone getting hurt." Her tone was soft but sure. "You know how important that is to me."

I opened my mouth, an argument on the tip of my tongue, but then closed it as I realized, with a sinking feeling, that it may not matter what I said. She wanted to do this and she was a grown woman. She didn't need my permission.

"Fine," I grumbled. "But I want you within ten feet of me at all times."

She squeezed my hand. "Thank you."

I held her gaze, biting back the urge to tell her how much I wished she'd just stay somewhere safe and quiet. I had to accept that wasn't what she wanted, and I couldn't drag her off like a caveman. It wasn't ten thousand B.C.

"Now that we've got that settled," Ronan said. "Sage,

would you mind sitting down with Fiona to make a list of everyone you remember from your father's past? Once that's done, I can ask around about them and Zeke can dig into their backgrounds digitally."

Sage nodded and got to her feet. "Should I come back in here when we're finished?"

"No, we'll be out in a minute."

"Okay." She left the office, closing the door behind herself.

Both Ronan and Zeke turned to me.

"What?" I asked, feeling like I was under a microscope.

"Are you sure you're still the best person to protect her?" Ronan asked, visibly uncomfortable.

"Of course." I shoved my chair back, insulted that he had to ask. "I'm the fucking director of personal security."

"Yes," he said slowly, "but you also have feelings for her."

My cheeks heated, and I glared at Zeke, who seemed to be enjoying this conversation far too much. "So what if I do?"

Ronan sighed. "I'm not questioning your abilities, but you can't afford to be distracted."

I leveled him with a look. "When Willow was in trouble, did you want anyone else watching her back?"

"Fuck, no." The answer came gratifyingly quickly.

"Well, that's how I feel about Sage." I made eye contact with him and then Zeke, holding for long enough that they'd know I was serious. "Nobody will keep her safer than me. I promise you that."

However much she might hate me for it, I'd give my life for her if I had to. In a heartbeat.

"Fine." Ronan's expression was full of misgiving. "But be careful."

"Hi." I stood in front of Fiona's desk, waiting for her to look away from her computer screen.

"I'll just be a sec." Her fingers moved furiously over the keyboard and she hit the enter button then looked up. "How are you doing?" Her eyes dipped to the bruises around my throat. "It must have been a hard day."

"It's been challenging, that's for sure." I smoothed my hands down the front of my shirt for lack of anything else to do with them. "Ronan has asked if we can put together a list of my father's old buddies."

"Okay." Fiona glanced around, then got up and grabbed a chair from a desk around the corner. "Sit here. I'll pull up a document."

I sat and for the next ten minutes, I listed every person I could remember Dad bringing home and every name he might have mentioned in passing. Considering how long it had been, I couldn't be certain how accurate the list was, but hopefully it would give us a starting point.

"Anyone else you can think of?" Fiona asked. "Did he play sports or have hobbies?"

"He liked to watch games on TV, but he never played sport as far as I can remember. As for hobbies, playing pool at the pub and coming up with get-rich-quick schemes were the main ones, and neither of them are very useful for what we need."

"It would be worth checking out any pubs he used to frequent," Fiona said. "Bartenders hear a lot, and it's possible some of the same staff still work there."

"That's a good idea. He did have one particular favorite, Lucky Dan's. Perhaps Kade and I should see if it's still around."

"It's as good a starting place as any." She stopped typing and swiveled her chair around. Her lips pursed. "It's brave, what you're doing," she said. "It was courageous of you to testify against those men in court as well. You were only a kid, and nobody would have blamed you if you'd refused."

I fidgeted, uncomfortable with her praise. It wasn't the first time someone had said something like that to me, but it never got easier. "I just did what I thought was the right thing."

"Yeah, well." Fiona gave a half-hearted laugh. "A lot of people wouldn't."

I wracked my mind for a way to change the topic and landed on something I'd been meaning to ask. In Ronan's office, I'd noticed that Fiona hadn't seemed to like Zeke, and since Kade was also uncertain about the guy, that intrigued me.

"So, I know Ronan and Kade reasonably well, but not Zeke. What do you think of him?"

Her face instantly morphed into a scowl. "He's an ass."

"Oh." I hadn't expected her to be so direct.

She sighed and rolled her eyes. "If you're worried about his loyalty, you don't need to be. I might want to put poison ivy in his underpants sometimes, but he's excellent at his job and he'd never turn on Ronan."

"Thanks." That eased my mind somewhat. I did have to wonder though... if Kade didn't like him, and neither did Fiona, did others here feel the same? If so, that must be a lonely way for him to live.

Fiona smiled slyly. "Is there something between you and Kade? It looked like there might be, and he's not one to give that impression unless there's truth to it."

A happy glow filled my chest. "There is. I'm not sure where it's going yet, but I like him." I lowered my voice and leaned closer. "The marriage lines on our palms are very similar too."

Her eyes widened. "Is that so?"

I nodded. "Not that it necessarily means anything, but it's a positive sign, I think."

"Definitely." Fiona glanced left and right, then held out her hands, palms up. "Could you read mine?"

I grinned. "Of course."

I took each of her hands in mine and studied them one by one and then side by side for comparison. I frowned, unsure how much to say.

"What is it?" she asked nervously.

I pressed my lips together, then raised my eyes to hers. "You haven't had an easy life."

She looked stunned and stared at me for a few seconds before nodding slowly. "You're right. I haven't."

"Do you really want to know what I see?" I asked. "Keep in mind, it's open to interpretation. My reading may not be the same as someone else's."

"Tell me." She sounded strangely urgent.

"See this here?" I pointed to a break in one of the lines. "It looks to me as though you've either been through or are about to go through a massive upheaval."

Fiona looked disquieted, and I cursed myself. Perhaps I should have kept my mouth shut. But she'd asked, and people had a right to honesty.

"What—" Ronan's office door swung inward and she cut herself off.

Kade and Zeke stepped out. Zeke gave me a cheeky grin and arched an eyebrow at Fiona, whose cheeks colored. I dropped her hands.

"Fiona and I had an idea about where we could start following up with Dad's old friends," I told Kade.

"What's that?" he asked. I explained to him about the pub, Lucky Dan's.

When I'd finished, Zeke spoke. "According to Google, Lucky Dan's is still going strong. Good work, ladies."

Kade held out a hand to me. I took it and let him pull me to my feet. He dropped a chaste kiss on my lips. "Come on, before I remember how much I'd rather lock you in a safe house and throw away the key."

Despite his grumbling, I smiled. He cared, and I liked that.

I threaded my fingers through his. "Let's go, silent giant."

18

KADE

Lucky Dan's was a seedy bar in a downtrodden area. The paint was peeling and the windows were so dirty that it was nearly impossible to see inside. All of my instincts told me this wasn't the kind of place Sage belonged. I wanted to whisk her away. But to my surprise, she seemed perfectly at home as we entered. I'd expected her to be tense and nervous, since there was a possibility the pub was one of the places Getty and Baker planned to visit, but her shoulders remained relaxed. Only one patron—a greasy-haired man in his sixties—sat at the bar, watching a replay of a football game on TV.

The grizzled bartender glanced up as we approached. His mouth was open, revealing yellow teeth. His eyes locked on Sage and several emotions flashed through them. Joy, affection, then stone-cold fear. He masked his expression so quickly I doubted Sage had noticed, but I laid a hand on her back to stop her. There was no reason for him to be afraid unless Getty and Baker had already been here. I scanned the pub, double-checking for any sign of them, then studied the drunk at the bar once more to make sure he really was what he appeared to be.

"Well, if it isn't the sweetest girl I ever met." The bartender limped around the counter and opened his arms for a hug. He didn't seem to be armed so I removed my hand from Sage's back and gestured for her to go ahead.

"Hi, Dan." She smiled in greeting and gave him a quick hug. When Dan held on for a few beats too long, I took a step forward, but I noticed he was murmuring something into her ear. Sage pulled away, searching his face. Dan flicked his eyes toward a door behind the counter, then made his way slowly toward it. Sage began to follow, but I stopped her again and went first, my hand on the gun concealed at my hip.

Dan held the door open and I moved stealthily into the room beyond, half expecting an ambush. When I'd checked behind the door, I motioned for Sage to enter, and Dan closed the door behind her.

"You shouldn't have come," he said gruffly. "Not that I'm not happy to see you, but some guys were here earlier, asking about your old man." He grabbed a cane that was leaning against the wall and used it for support. "I didn't like the look of them. A couple of cold bastards, and they were carrying. You need to watch your back."

"They've been here?" Sage asked. "One short guy, and the other with blue eyes?"

Dan inclined his head. "That's them. Doesn't take a genius to know those two are trouble." He jerked his chin toward me. "Who's this?"

"Kade is keeping me safe," she told him. "He's former special forces."

Dan turned assessing eyes on me. "I hope you know what you're doing. These guys aren't playing around. I got the feeling they'd happily have gutted me if they thought I knew anything useful." He heaved a sigh and gave Sage his attention once more. "I know your father was a useless layabout, but you were the most precious thing in his world, and he'd want you to stay away from that lot. If I were you, I'd skip town for a while."

Sage's throat bobbled as she swallowed. "I know he did," she whispered. "But the men who are after me have broken out of prison, and we need to make sure they're locked away again."

Dan's expression was grim, but he nodded. "Have you talked to Mick? You know how close he and your dad were."

Sage and I exchanged a glance.

"We haven't yet," she said. "But maybe we'll do that next."

"Good idea." Dan scanned me from head to toe. "I hope you've got a gun."

"I do."

"That's something, I guess."

"If they come back, make sure they know she's protected," I ordered.

"If they come back, I'll be greeting them with a shotgun," Dan grumbled. "They caught me off guard last time, but it won't happen again." He hobbled to Sage and kissed her cheek. "Take care of yourself, and give me a call to let me know you're still alive."

She pressed her lips together and, for the first time today, tears shone in her eyes. "I will. Thanks, Dan."

"Anytime, kid."

We left the back room and rounded the bar.

"Wait a sec," Dan called. He scribbled something on a piece of paper and stuffed it into Sage's hand. "Take this."

She smiled and nodded. When we were back outside, she unscrunched the paper. I shifted closer so we could both see what it said. All the note contained was a name, Mick Trembley, and an address.

"Good old Dan," Sage said. "Should we go there now?"

"Might as well." If this Mick guy had been close to Sage's father, perhaps he'd have the answers we needed. "Let's go."

I ushered her into the car and plugged the address into the GPS, then followed the directions to a rundown apartment block with barred windows on the first floor. It wasn't the sort of place I'd want to take Sage into under any circumstances, let alone when a pair of killers were hunting her, but the determination in her eyes told me there was no point trying to stop her, so I got out of the car and rested one hand lightly on the butt of my gun.

"Let's get this over with."

―――――

SAGE

As Kade and I climbed a short flight of stairs to the first floor, where Mick supposedly lived, something from our conversation with Dan niggled at the back of my mind. I couldn't put my finger on what it was—a word he'd used or a phrase that had triggered a memory—but I knew it was important. I tried to grasp at the trailing thought and follow it, but couldn't get anywhere. Perhaps I could meditate on it later and see what came up.

Kade stopped outside an apartment. "It's this one."

He rapped on the door and positioned himself protectively beside me. I heard scuffing inside, then the rattle of a chain in a lock. Eventually, the door opened and a pair of rheumy eyes looked into mine. My stomach dropped. Mick had never been the picture of health, having smoked like a chimney and drunk like a duck, but I'd never seen him as such an empty husk of a human being as he looked now. His eyes were blank, his skin sallow and creased, and he was clearly having trouble recognizing me.

"It's Sage," I told him. "Sage Nichols."

His expression brightened. "Brendan's girl. You've grown so much, I couldn't tell who you were."

"It's been a while." I hadn't seen him since Dad's funeral.

"So it has." He made no move to ask us in, and I shifted from one foot to the other, wondering how to wrangle an invitation.

"Can we come in?" Kade said bluntly. I winced. Mick had never responded well to people being pushy with him.

Mick's bushy eyebrows lowered and he made a phlegmy sound in the back of his throat. "I don't know who you are, and I don't want you in my home." He waved a hand at me. "She can come in. You can stay there."

Kade stiffened, and I guessed he was thinking how easily something could happen to me if I was out of his sight.

Before he could refuse and risk alienating Mick, I decided to suggest an alternative. "How about you wait in the doorway, Kade, and I'll step inside with Mick?"

His expression darkened. "I don't like it."

"I'll stay near to you," I promised. "It might be safer than standing in the corridor anyway."

He grimaced but I could tell he could see the sense in what I'd said. "Okay, but if I get the slightest sense something is off, we're out of here."

I mock saluted him. "Yes, sir."

Mick rolled his eyes and shuffled backward. "Come on. I got better things to do than get glared at by your boyfriend."

I started to say he wasn't my boyfriend, but then stopped. Maybe he was. We hadn't had a conversation about our relationship, but I didn't have sex with people lightly. I had no problem with anyone who did, but it wasn't my thing. My heart told me he was the same, and that what we'd shared meant something. I glanced at his scowly face and saw his eyes soften as they landed on me. My tummy flipped over. Yeah, this was something worth holding on to.

I perched on the edge of a saggy armchair just inside the door and waited while Mick grabbed a half-empty bottle of beer and collapsed onto the sofa. As he scratched the back of his head, I noticed track marks down the inside of his arm and my stomach sunk even more. Many of them were old, but some were clearly fresh. He saw where I was looking and dropped his arm to his side.

"Has anyone come asking questions about Dad recently?" I asked, to get the ball rolling.

"Nah. I haven't heard the name Brendan Nichols in years. Why?"

I debated how much to tell him. While Dad and Mick had been close, the man was clearly unwell and I had no way of knowing how trustworthy he'd be. "Someone is trying to find the money he stole," I said, settling for a partial truth. There was no need to tell him the men in question were the ones who'd killed Dad and escaped prison. "I thought they might have come looking for you in case you have any idea where he put it."

Mick chortled wetly. "You think I'd be living in a shithole like this if I had any idea where the money was?" He shook his head. "I spent weeks looking for that cash. Figured if anyone could find it, it'd be me, but there was no sign of the damn stuff."

Kade scoffed in the doorway and I shot him a look. Mick would hardly open up to us if he knew Kade was silently judging him.

"Where did you look?" I asked.

Mick rested his head against the back of the sofa and closed his eyes as if trying to summon the memory. "I didn't bother with your house since the cops had already tossed it, but I snooped around his gym, his favorite pubs, your school, that canning factory he used to work at, and badgered every friend of his I could think of. I even checked the garden in case he'd buried it." He opened his eyes and leaned forward. "I'm telling you, he made that money disappear. My best guess is he rented a safety deposit box under an alias. I asked around but no one at those secure storage places would admit to seeing him."

I sighed in disappointment. I hadn't expected Mick to have all the answers, but I'd hoped for more than we'd gotten. I studied him, sorrow pervading me. He seemed like a lonely, sick man who was old beyond his years. If my father had lived, would he have ended up like this? He and Mom had been on the rocks. It was possible they would have divorced. It made me sad to wonder.

"Do you know if anyone else was looking for the money?" Kade asked from the doorway.

Mick's rheumy gaze flicked to him, and he shrugged. "Probably all of us, but nobody was saying a damn thing."

From his tone, I got the impression we wouldn't be hearing much more from Mick.

"Is there anything you need?" I asked softly.

He choked out a laugh. "Another kidney. A few thousand dollars."

My lips twisted. "I can't help you there, sorry."

"Nah, I didn't think so." With a grunt of effort, he pushed himself to his feet. "Off with you, then."

"Bye, Mick."

"Yeah, yeah." He ushered us to the door, then shut it firmly behind us.

Kade raised a brow. "Your dad was friends with him?"

I took his hand, surprised—and a little pleased—when he immediately interlaced his fingers with mine. "Dad was a complicated guy."

He snorted. "That's putting it mildly." He scanned the corridor, which was still empty. "People are listening."

I nodded, and we left the building without speaking another word. Outside, darkness was beginning to descend.

"Time to go to the safe house." Kade's tone brooked no argument.

"Sure." I needed time to process everything I'd seen and done and heard today.

I got into the passenger seat and he drove to an apartment building about three or four blocks from where Willow and Ronan lived in Ronan's penthouse. From the outside, the place was nicer than either of the other two safe houses we'd used, and when he escorted me inside, the decor was pleasant and modern.

"Any thoughts on where to start tomorrow?" Kade asked as we took the elevator up.

I sorted through the possibilities but didn't land on anything that felt promising. "Maybe we could visit the house."

He jerked in surprise. "Your old house, you mean?"

"Yeah." I bit my lip. "Being there might help me remember something important."

"Are you sure you can handle it?"

"I'll be okay, if you're there with me. We need answers, and it's probably the best way to knock something loose."

He hesitated. "They might have it under surveillance."

"Then we'll take precautions." Now that I'd settled on the idea, it felt like the right thing to do.

"I don't like it." He sounded frustrated. "I want you safe."

"I know." I stepped into his embrace and gazed up at him. "But I'll have you with me, and I know I'm safe with you."

He ducked his head to kiss me. "Always."

19

I both loved and hated Sage's faith in me. As I drew her close and deepened the kiss, I knew that I'd do everything it took to protect her, but I was still only one man, and I wasn't invincible.

The elevator pinged and the doors glided open. I pulled away, forcing myself to ignore her flushed cheeks and dilated pupils in favor of scanning the corridor for threats. Near the end of the hall, two men stood outside an apartment. I recognized the taller of the pair as Sean. I stepped out of the elevator and kept one hand on Sage's waist and the other on my gun as we walked the length of the corridor. The safe house was the last apartment on the right, and I nodded to the guards as we approached.

"Everything is secure," Sean reported. "Zeke came by to check for spyware and nobody other than us has been here. The apartments above and below are both empty. A deaf old lady lives in the apartment to the right. We knocked on the door earlier and she could barely hear a word we said. She's not a threat."

"Thanks." Sean passed me a key and I slotted it into the lock. "What time are you on duty until?"

"Ten, and then another two will replace us. Lyle is inside. He'll patrol the interior so you can rest."

"Great." I'd rather have Sage to myself, but I knew Lyle would keep quiet, and I really did need to get a decent sleep so it would be good to have him there. "Talk later."

I pushed the apartment door open, and peered around it, cataloging furniture that could have come straight from a showroom. A tall, broad-shouldered blond man stood by the window on the opposite wall, at attention.

He dipped his head in greeting. "Sir."

"Lyle," I replied. "Thanks for coming in."

"No problem, sir. Just so you know, there's a fire exit through this window. There are two other windows, one in a bedroom and the other in the bathroom, but neither can be easily accessed and both are locked. I'll keep an eye on this one and check the others intermittently."

"Sounds good. Continue."

We took a left turn out of the living room into the hall. The two bedrooms that came off it were tastefully decorated and smelled faintly of vanilla. I wondered briefly if the apartment had come fully furnished or if someone from the team had enjoyed spending the company's money on nice trappings. I didn't care enough to ask though. I grabbed the pillow from one room and took it into the other.

"We're sharing," I announced. "I don't want any more nasty nighttime surprises."

Sage smiled. "I'd like to sleep with you regardless of the danger."

My heart pitter-pattered dangerously. "I'd like to do more than sleep."

The corners of her eyes crinkled. "Let's find something to eat first."

I sighed. "If we have to."

We returned to the living area. In the kitchen, we found ingredients for burgers and worked together to make a massive cheeseburger for me and a halloumi burger for Sage. After we'd eaten, she asked if I'd mind if she did a meditation. I sat on the sofa and she lay with her head on my lap and her eyes closed. She breathed deeply and evenly.

I watched the rise and fall of her chest, then finally allowed myself to indulge in a shameless visual exploration of her face. She was so beautiful I couldn't look at her without something pinching in the vicinity of my chest. Her dark eyelashes contrasted sharply with the milky color of her skin. Her lips were slightly parted and I yearned to run my thumb over the plush shape of them. Her chin was fine but strong, and her nose was small and slightly upturned. The corners of her mouth turned upward into a slight smile, stealing my breath. I glanced at Lyle to see if he'd noticed how captivated I was by her, but he was studiously looking the other way.

We stayed like that until my thighs started to go numb. I considered whether to shift her, but she seemed so peaceful. I frowned, noticing that her breaths had fallen into a soft, natural rhythm. I stifled a laugh. She was asleep.

Gathering her against my chest, I stood and carried her to the bedroom. She stirred and murmured something, but I shushed her and placed her gently on the bed. She rolled onto her side and curled up, letting out a contented murmur. The sight tugged at my gut. I stripped off my clothes and got in behind her. As she snuggled into my embrace, I couldn't help thinking about how much I'd like this to be permanent. Not the situation, but going to sleep with Sage in my arms. I wanted to do this every night. To be able to hold her and shower her with all the love and affection she deserved but had never had.

I brushed her hair off her forehead and kissed her temple. For the first time, I allowed myself to dream of a life with her in it, and it was beautiful.

SAGE

I awoke to the sound of groaning. Beside me, Kade was thrashing in his sleep, his face twisted in distress. He must be dreaming. I was sure he had plenty of fodder from his real life to fuel awful nightmares.

"Hey, now." I stroked his arm, being careful not to encroach too much on his space in case he lashed out. "It's okay. I'm here." He threw his head back, his expression pained, and I wondered whether I should wake him. "I'm right here," I repeated. "You're not alone."

I continued smoothing my hands over his arms and shoulders until he eventually stilled.

"Sage?" His voice rasped in the quiet between us.

"Everything is okay," I told him. "You had a nightmare."

He sat up and dragged his hands down his face. "Sorry if I woke you."

"Don't be." I shifted closer to him. "I've had plenty of sleep already. I'm glad I was able to help."

He ran a hand through his hair, and even in the dim light, I could see the tips were standing on end. "It's nothing new. I have nightmares pretty much every week, and when I wake up, I'm always too shaken to sleep again."

I gnawed on my lip, wondering how much to pry. "Do you want to talk about it?"

He sighed and cupped my face, his aim unerring even in

the darkness. "No. I'd rather you distract me with something more pleasant."

My lips tugged up. He was avoiding the topic, but considering I had a pretty good idea what his nightmares were about, I saw no reason not to indulge him. After all, we were both awake and nobody would expect us to be up for hours yet. I leaned forward and touched my mouth to his, then flicked my tongue over his lips and felt a rumble in his chest.

"Do you think you can be quiet?" I asked. "Lyle will still be in the living area."

He captured my lips again, and heat pooled at the apex of my thighs. "I'm having a really hard time caring what Lyle hears when you taste so good."

"Ugh, I still have all my clothes on," I complained.

"I didn't want to disturb you." He grabbed the hem of my shirt and lifted it over my head.

I made short work of the bra and took off my yoga bottoms and panties, then straddled his lap. He must have also shucked off his clothes because his firm cock pushed insistently against my sex. I shivered in pleasure and rocked my hips, sliding along the length of him. Kade settled one hand on the small of my back. His touch felt possessive and I instinctively edged closer. Strong fingers gripped my chin and our mouths met in a hot, wild kiss. He grabbed my ass and encouraged me to ride his erection. I whimpered as the head of his cock bumped against my clit over and over again. Kade kissed me, smothering the sounds.

"Quiet," he reminded me.

I wrapped my legs around his waist, crossing my ankles behind his back, and used the leverage to quicken my pace. He was driving me crazy, and I wanted to do the same to him. He grunted and tightened his grip so I couldn't move.

I brushed my mouth over the shell of his ear. "Quiet," I murmured.

He trembled, and a dark thrill went through me, unlike anything I'd ever felt. Kade swung his legs off the edge of the bed and lifted me. I squeaked in surprise. He rifled around in the dark and held something in front of me. A foil wrapper.

"I like the way you think." I took the condom from him and when he gently deposited me on the bed, I tore it open, encircled his shaft with my fingers and thumb, and slid it on. He positioned himself behind me and wrapped me in his strong embrace. I snuggled closer, loving the way he felt around me, and how safe it seemed in the circle of his arms.

He kissed the side of my neck, then lifted one of my thighs. My eyes widened as I realized his intention, and I helped guide his cock inside me, biting my lower lip as he filled me from behind.

He made love to me with steady thrusts. I gave myself to the moment, allowing my limbs to become languid. I was pinned against his chest so there was nothing I could do except indulge in the decadence of this stolen moment with him. He curved his calloused hand around one of my breasts and toyed with the nipple, then splayed it over my lower belly, two of his fingers pressing against my clit.

"Kade," I gasped, trapped between his fingers and his cock, sensation overwhelming me.

"Let go," he murmured against my hair. "I've got you."

"Feels so good."

"I know, baby. You're incredible."

Desire was thick in his voice as his fingers played against me, never letting up. I arched, wound so tight that all it took was the whisper of his breath over the nape of my neck for my entire world to shatter. Red-hot pleasure blazed through me and I heard myself cry out. Then Kade stiffened and pulsed inside me.

Neither of us moved until the sweat began to cool on my skin and Kade's softening cock slipped out of me. With a grunt of effort, he got up and cleaned himself off, then returned with a cloth and tenderly wiped down my body. We slipped beneath the blankets together and he held me until I drifted back to sleep. I didn't know what the morning would bring, but for now, I didn't really care.

20

SAGE

"Are you sure you want to do this?" Kade asked for the umpteenth time as he navigated the streets between the safe house and my teenage home. "The police have turned it over. Any clues about where he put the money are probably gone."

I nodded, even though my stomach was tangled up and I thought I might be sick. "Yeah. I told you, it's not about the clues. It's about triggering a memory."

His lips pursed. "Are we sure that 'triggering' is something we want to do to you?"

I looked at him out of the corner of my eye and covered my mouth to hide a smile. He was trying to protect me, and that was sweet, but sometimes we needed to revisit our trauma in order to be cleansed. While I had no doubt the visit would stir up memories I'd rather not relive, I also knew it wouldn't send me into a tailspin the way he feared. I was stronger than that.

I reached for his hand, loving the way he instinctively intertwined his fingers with mine. "Tell you what. Why don't you focus on the physical threats and I'll worry about the emotional stuff?"

He shot me a narrow-eyed look. "Fine, I can take a hint."

I smiled again as I released his hand. If it weren't for the specter of Getty and Baker hanging over us, I'd be having a pretty perfect day. Morning sex with a gorgeous man, followed by napping, and the luxury of making a green smoothie for breakfast because whatever wonderful person had stocked the apartment had made sure I had everything I'd need. I hummed to myself as we drove, realizing we weren't far away now.

The house was in a nice neighborhood. In hindsight, I should have wondered how we afforded it, but teenage me hadn't considered how expensive our lifestyle might be—at least relative to Mom's income level. If I had questioned it, would things have turned out differently? Perhaps we could have had a conversation about finances, and I could have made it clear to Dad that being on the right side of the law, and having him safe, meant more to me than owning the latest fashions and going to the best schools. Ah well, too late for those 'what ifs' now.

Kade turned a corner and there it was, up ahead of us.

"That one," I said, pointing at it.

He pulled over and paused to check out a black Ford parked on the opposite side of the quiet suburban street. "They're cops."

I leaned closer to the window to get a better look and noticed that there were two people seated inside, a man and a woman. "How can you tell?"

"The model of the car. The fact there are two of them. It wouldn't surprise me if Jo put them here in case Getty and Baker turn up."

"Will they stop us from going in?" I asked.

He glanced at me. "Of course not. It's your house. But

they'll probably take notes, and maybe a couple of photos. They might approach us if they want to know what we're doing. Be prepared for questions."

"Okay."

He got out of the car and I waited while he surveyed the area and came around to help me. We followed a path across the small front lawn, which had been mowed recently. One of the neighbors must be doing outdoor maintenance since I doubted the police had concerned themselves with taking care of the property. Even if they had, full access had technically been returned to me now, and the police no longer cared what happened to it.

I searched my purse for the key and slotted it into the lock. Kade ushered me aside, turned the key, and gently pushed the door open. The house was silent. He stepped inside, one hand on his gun, which I figured was more of a safety measure than out of any real expectation that someone would be here. The cops would surely have intervened if they'd seen an intruder.

When he beckoned for me to follow, I placed one foot on the carpeted floor and inhaled the musty scent of disuse. I looked ahead at the entrance to the living room, and my vision wavered. Voices seemed to travel to my ears through the fog of time. My mom and dad, arguing. I blinked, and when I opened my eyes again, it was as if I was there. My heart beat frantically against my ribcage as I tiptoed along the floor, drawn by the sound of ghosts.

What if I'd opened that door and confronted them?

What if I'd asked what was wrong?

I rested my fingertips against the wood, concentrating on everything I'd thought, smelled, seen, and heard at the time. I knew it was crazy, but I almost felt as though I could push the door open and see my parents standing on the other side.

I couldn't bring myself to do it. Not when I knew I'd see a crime scene. Instead, I backtracked to my former bedroom. The bedding had been torn off, the mattress slashed, and the dresser drawers were open, my clothes spilling out.

A sob rose up my throat and I lifted a shaking hand to my mouth as I took in the damage. The evidence of a police search was obvious, from the open closet to the upturned nightstand, but I suspected someone else was responsible for the mattress. Perhaps one of Dad's former acquaintances. My shoulders shook with emotion and I closed my eyes and forced myself to take deep, slow breaths, relieved when Kade slung an arm around me. Seeing this place, which had once been my safe space, trashed like this made me feel violated. Even more so than when Getty and Baker had broken into my house.

I was tempted to chant a protection spell and envision a beautiful, pure orb of light around me that would keep me distanced from the ruin, but if I wanted to remember something important, I couldn't shield myself. I had to just let whatever may come, come.

"You all right?" Kade asked gruffly.

"Not really," I admitted. "But I will be."

I took his hand and made myself register every detail, then I crossed the hall to my parents' room. Like mine, their bed had been torn apart and their belongings were tossed haphazardly about. I was almost grateful for it. If the room had been untouched, it would have been easy to imagine them sleeping in the bed, waiting for me to return.

I wandered around, stepping over debris, and when I'd soaked up everything I could, I went to the living room door. This time, I turned the handle and pushed it open. Dust stirred in the air, and my gaze was immediately drawn to the spot where Mom had last lain on the floor, bleeding and broken. There was a neat hole in the carpet, where the bloodstain had been cut out by the police in case they needed to use it as evidence.

My pulse pounded wildly as I slowly raised my eyes to the edge of the hearth. A small, rust-colored smudge was all that was left to show where Mom had hit her head. Clinging to Kade like a lifeline, I paced over to the hole in the carpet and sunk to my knees. He dropped with me, murmuring words of comfort. I didn't notice I was crying until a tear hit the exposed boards. I sobbed soundlessly, and Kade cradled me to his chest. I squeezed my eyes shut, glad he was here with me. In a short time, he'd become my rock. Eventually, I ran out of tears, and he helped me to my feet, keeping an arm around me for support.

I sniffed. "This is where they fought."

He nodded. "I'm sorry."

"Yeah." My throat felt so tight, it was uncomfortable to speak. "Come on. I want to see the backyard."

KADE

I'd never been superstitious, but something in the bones of this place felt wrong. If I were a spiritual man, I might think it was cursed or that too much blood had stained the floors and a sense of pain lingered in the air all these years later.

It was on the tip of my tongue to ask Sage if she was ready to face the backyard, or if she'd rather we go out front and get some air, but I knew I needed to trust her to take the lead. I nodded and let her guide me through a dining room and past a kitchen with dirty dishes in the sink as though someone had merely stepped away for a few hours. It gave me the chills.

Sage unlatched the deadbolt on the back door. The

hinges creaked as she drew the door open and we both flinched, my hand leaping immediately to my gun. A couple of concrete steps went down from the doorstep to the lawn. She took them one at a time, then stopped and stared into space. I didn't bother trying to follow her gaze because I knew she was seeing something that wasn't there.

"I came outside," she said quietly. "Dad had a gun."

"That must have frightened you."

"Yes." She swayed, and I steadied her. "I ran behind the shed." She retraced her steps and I kept pace with her, walking along the side of a rickety shed and around to the rear, where there were several holes in the boards. "I climbed here and looked over." She marched to the end of the shed and gazed back into the yard. "I saw them. Baker was in the center, with Parrish and LaMond on either side. Then Getty came out of the house."

Another tear tracked down her cheek, and she shook her head. "I ducked and got far enough away to call 911. I didn't see anything else, but I heard them shoot his kneecap when he wouldn't give them answers. Not long after that, the police arrived and I heard more shots. I was so scared." Her voice cracked. "I just hid over there like a terrified child. I've tried to forgive myself for being a coward. I probably couldn't have done anything to help even if I'd been brave enough to try, but I'll always wonder."

A heaviness weighed on my chest. I couldn't stand the thought of what she'd been through. I hated that she felt guilty for not doing more, but I understood it because I felt the same way for failing to protect Charlotte. Logically, I knew it wasn't my fault she'd died—it wasn't even my friend's fault for letting her down. The responsibility lay firmly in the hands of her rapist. But in my heart, I'd never believed it, and likewise, nothing I could say would release

Sage's sense of guilt. She was the only person who could forgive herself.

"I'm glad you survived." It was the only thing I could think to say. "I'm sure your dad would be too. He wanted you to run. He wanted you to be safe."

She pressed her lips together, but there was no mistaking her expression for a smile. "Sometimes I get so angry with him I can hardly breathe. If he hadn't stolen that money, none of this would have happened. But not all of my fury is aimed at him. If I'd chosen to go to a cheaper college, or if I hadn't hidden like a coward, who knows how things might be different."

I had nothing to say to that so we stood in silence for several minutes until Sage released a pent-up breath and seemed to pull herself together.

"Do you want to have a look around?" she asked. "I'm sure the place has been well-searched over the years, but we might find something everyone else missed."

"Sure." I stuffed my hands into my pockets and followed as she strode determinedly back inside.

We worked methodically through each room in the house, picking up the things on the floor and shaking them out, checking inside drawers and the pockets of clothing, and rifling through the linen cupboard and pantry. I opened the refrigerator and an overwhelming stench of rot blasted me in the face. I gasped, my eyes watering, and scanned the shelves as quickly as possible before slamming it shut.

"How do we get to the attic and basement?" I asked after we'd searched all the obvious places.

"There's a door to the basement beside the cupboard with the bedding in it," Sage said. "Access to the attic is via a pull-down ladder in the living room."

We returned to the basement door. When I tried the

handle, it stuck, so I used my pocketknife to lever it open. The basement was dark, and it smelled dank.

"Are you sure you want to go down there?" Sage asked hesitantly.

"Yeah." I withdrew my weapon. "I want you to stay here and keep guard with your gun in your hands. If anyone comes while I'm gone, shoot first and ask questions later."

When she was in position, I switched on the flashlight app on my phone and made my way cautiously down the stairs. I circled the flashlight around me, noting with disappointment that the space was empty. I paced around the entire area anyway to see whether anything seemed to have been disturbed. It was a bust. So was the attic, and the garden shed.

"I have one last idea," I told Sage, picking up a tool kit on the way out of the shed. In the bathroom, I disconnected the vanity piping and checked inside it, then did the same with the kitchen. Finally, I opened the toilet cistern. No sign of anything in the plumbing. "Damn."

Sage huffed in frustration. "I have this feeling there's something I'm not remembering, but I can't put my finger on it. I'm sorry it's been a wasted visit."

I kissed her cheek. "It hasn't been a waste. No investigation ever is. It's just another option we've ruled out."

She leaned into the shelter of my body and sighed. "Thanks for saying that. So, what now?"

"Now, we're going to do something a bit different."

She looked up at me, frowning. "Like what?"

I kissed her pouting lips. "You'll see."

I'd had the idea in the early hours of the morning, after she'd returned to sleep but I hadn't been able to. Hopefully it would take her mind off everything that being here had stirred up.

21

———

SAGE

I was curious what Kade had in mind as we exited the house, locked up, and got back into the car, but I was also exhausted, so I rested my forehead against the window and closed my eyes. The movement of the vehicle lulled me as Kade drove back the way we'd come, but when he made a turn I wasn't expecting, I blinked rapidly and sat up. We were nearing a familiar block of shops. My stomach lurched as he pulled over beside one of the buildings.

"What's going on?" I asked, bemused.

He smiled, affection shining in his eyes. "I thought after the morning we've had, you might want to visit somewhere that holds good memories for you, and we're already in the area."

"I can't believe you brought me here." I gazed out the window, into the shop where I used to while away hours among the crystals, listening to soft music. "This is where I first learned yoga."

"I remember."

My heart felt so full it might burst. "Thank you. This is one of the nicest things anyone has ever done for me."

Tears once again prickled in my eyes, but this time, they were good tears. I patted them away, met Kade's eyes, and smiled tremulously. He was such a wonderful man, and I was falling deeper in love with him each day. I couldn't think of anyone else who would have made such a thoughtful gesture. It showed that he listened and cared.

"Do you want to go in?" he asked.

"Yes." I got out and my feet carried me inside on autopilot. I was barely aware of Kade striding alongside me, vigilant as ever.

A chime tinkled as we entered and the familiar scent of floral incense greeted us. I breathed it in and closed my eyes as a sense of homecoming washed over me. A pan flute was playing over the speakers and there was a hush that was cozy but not oppressive. I opened my eyes and looked around. The crystals were displayed in the same part of the shop they always had been, but a new water feature had been installed in one corner. I sat on the bench beside the small pond, closed my eyes, and focused on clearing my mind. I sensed movement, but not nearby. Kade was giving me space.

I don't know how long I stayed that way, but when I brought myself back to the present, I had to blink as my eyes readjusted to the light. Kade stood near the counter, speaking softly to a woman with long gray hair held back by a bandanna. I'd recognize her anywhere.

"Joy!" I exclaimed.

A smile lit Joy's pixie-like features. "I was just telling your friend how glad I am you've come to visit."

I hurried over and threw my arms around her. "It's so good to see you."

"The same to you, blossom. It's been too long, but I've been keeping an eye on you online. I like to be able to tell people that Sage Nichols first studied yoga with me."

Pleasure suffused me and I released her. I turned to Kade. "Joy taught me everything I know."

Joy gave a tinkling laugh. "No, blossom. I simply guided you along a short part of your journey."

I kissed her cheek. "It was so much more than that. You gave me peace when I needed it."

"And now you do the same for thousands of others." She smiled contentedly. "The circle of life continues."

Kade glanced from Joy to me and smiled in bemusement.

"Let me get you a herbal infusion and we can talk," Joy said. "If you have time?"

I met Kade's eyes and he nodded. "That sounds perfect," I said.

Joy prepared our drinks and cleared chairs in the corner for us to sit in. She offered a small bowl of nuts and seeds as a snack and we chatted easily about the shop, my yoga classes and social media pages, and the people we both knew. By the time we left, I'd promised to return soon to teach one of her yoga classes, and I was feeling more grounded than I had in a long time.

KADE

As we were exiting Joy's shop, a guy with blue-tinted hair was about to enter. He took one look at Sage and stopped in his tracks.

"Sage?" he demanded, loudly enough to draw attention from passers-by. "Sage Nichols, is that you?"

I wrapped a protective arm around Sage's shoulder. She'd stiffened and was staring at the blue-haired man with apprehension. Tension seemed to zing back and forth between them and I didn't like it one bit.

"Who are you?" I demanded.

His eyes flicked to me but didn't linger.

"Guy." Sage didn't sound nearly as pleased to see him as he was to see her.

"Let's get out of the doorway," I suggested, steering Sage aside and hoping the other man might leave us alone. No such luck. He followed, keeping pace until we stopped.

"I can't believe it's really you." Guy gestured up and down the length of Sage's body as though she was some kind of apparition. "Have you been to see Joy?" He waved a hand dismissively. "Never mind, of course you have. I'm surprised you have time for the little people these days. I thought it would all be brunch and spa sessions with other influencers."

Sage edged closer to me, and I narrowed my eyes at the interloper. It was clear they had some kind of history and I didn't want to overstep, but I also didn't like her reaction to him. "It's not that glamorous," she said in a tone I'd have called sulky from anyone else, but I'd never heard anything like it from her. "Yoga and social media pay the bills, but I mostly keep to myself. I'm not living the lifestyle of the rich and famous."

Guy laughed. "Of course not. That's never been your style." He shook his head. "You look incredible."

He reached for one of her hands, but she snatched it away. I frowned. It was unlike Sage to avoid someone like this. Should I step in?

"By the way, I've always wanted to tell you how brave I think you were for acting as a witness in court," Guy said. "That was so strong of you."

Finally, Sage seemed to find her tongue. She took a step forward, her eyes flashing with a rare moment of temper. "As opposed to you, who bailed as soon as things got hard?"

Guy raised his hands defensively. "It wasn't like that. I

was a kid, and we were probably going to break up when you went to that dramatic arts college anyway. I just sped things along."

Sage thrust her chin forward. "You abandoned me when my parents died and I needed support. I was a kid, too."

"But that wasn't my fault," he protested. "It's not like I expected what happened. Your dad was involved in some shady stuff."

Oh hell, no.

"Get lost," I growled. If I was reading this right, and this asshole had broken up with Sage right after her parents died, I didn't want him within ten feet of her. Preferably a hundred.

Guy swallowed and took a nervous step back. "This doesn't have anything to do with you."

I grabbed Sage's hand and raised it to my lips, staring him down. "Yes, it does, because I'm the man who takes care of Sage, and unless she tells me otherwise, that means getting her away from a shit like you."

He lowered his gaze from mine and focused on Sage instead. "I can't believe you're with this Neanderthal."

"He's a good man." Her voice, strong and sure, made me want to beat on my chest. "He won't leave me because of a little inconvenience, and I'm pretty sure he's serious, so you'd better walk away."

Guy scowled and stormed away, stomping past the shop without going in.

I pulled Sage into my arms and she sagged against me.

"I shouldn't have said those things to him," she sighed. "I'm meant to have forgiven him."

I kissed the top of her head. It seemed there were a lot of things she was meant to have forgiven, but good intentions could only go so far. Some emotional wounds lingered no matter how much you tried to cover them up.

"He made you angry. You're only human."

"I should be better." She sounded disappointed in herself.

I drew back far enough that I could look down into her face. The happy shine that had been in her eyes during our time in the shop had disappeared, and she was worrying her lower lip with her teeth.

"You are the best person I know," I told her. "But you're not a robot. You're allowed to feel your feelings."

"I know." Her expression became wry. "I just thought I was done with that."

"I don't think we ever really stop working through things."

"I'm sure you're right." She pursed her lips. "Anyway, that was Guy. He's the reason trust is so important to me in relationships. We were dating when Mom and Dad were killed, and he dropped me as soon as it became clear what a mess the situation was."

Fury tore through me at the thought of someone abandoning Sage in her time of need. I had to pause to remind myself that if he'd stuck by her, I might not have had the chance to be with her now.

"That's fucked up," I said. "He didn't deserve you."

"No, he didn't," she agreed with a small smile.

I ignored the internal voice that said I didn't deserve her either, and kissed her mouth gently once more.

"I think that's enough excitement for one morning. Let's head back to the safe house to regroup."

22

KADE

I took as many back roads as I could on the way to the safe house, figuring that would help us fly under the radar. We were ten minutes from our destination when my phone vibrated in my pocket. I grabbed it and, seeing it was my mother, decided I'd better answer.

"Can you accept the call and put it on speaker?" I asked Sage.

"Sure." She hit a couple of buttons and then Mom's voice filled the car.

"Where are you?" she demanded in an unusually snappish tone.

"Working," I replied.

"Can you get away?" she asked.

Something in her voice gave me pause. "Why?"

"Audrey has been injured in action. I've only just heard. She's been treated overseas and is being transferred to the local hospital as we speak."

"She's here?" Last I'd known, Audrey had been deployed somewhere in the Middle East.

"Yes. Apparently they've done as much as they can for her and now she's being sent home to recover."

"What happened?" For them to have sent her back stateside, it must be serious.

"I don't know!" Mom wailed. "They wouldn't tell me details. I'm going to see her. I need to make sure my baby is all right."

Guilt wormed into my gut. I'd always felt responsible for Audrey's decision to join the military, but this was the first time she'd been seriously injured. There was no saying how bad it might be. Her life could be on the line simply because she'd idolized me when we were younger.

I gritted my teeth. "I'm sure she's okay," I lied. "I'll be there as soon as I can. Can you text me the details?"

"I'll do that now."

"Thanks. And Mom, don't drive yourself. You're in no state to be behind the wheel."

She sniffed. "I know. I've already called Cathy to come and get me."

Cathy was my aunt.

"That's great. I've got to go now, but I'll see you soon."

She said goodbye and hung up.

I glanced at Sage and cursed, wracking my brain for options. I couldn't leave her on her own. I'd have to arrange for someone else to guard her, but I hated the thought of trusting anyone to take care of her. I couldn't stand to lose her. But unfortunately, I wouldn't be any good to her until I knew what the situation with Audrey was. I'd be too distracted.

"Go straight to the hospital," she said, as if reading my thoughts.

I shook my head. "I'll drop you off at the safe house first. The guys there can guard you."

"Kade." She laid her hand on my thigh. "Take me with

you to the hospital. Your family needs you. Don't waste any time."

I grimaced. "I won't be able to clear it properly."

"Call one of the guards from the safe house and they can join us. That way, I'll have someone with me while you're with your mom and sister. They need you more than I do right now."

The discomfort in my gut eased. I did like the idea of keeping her close to me, but this would hardly be ideal. It wasn't by the book and there was a good chance Ronan would disapprove, but it was the only option I felt like I could live with.

"Okay," I conceded. "Call Sean and ask him to meet us there. Until he arrives, you need to be within sight at all times." Something heavy caught in my chest. "You're too important to risk."

Her smile made my insides feel sweet and smooth as molasses. "Whatever you need."

I watched with amazement as she got the address and room number from Mom and plugged it into the GPS to find the fastest route, then called Sean to make arrangements. When everything was organized, she dug into her purse and withdrew a translucent white stone, which she clasped on her lap.

"I'm going to send her healing energy," she said, closing her eyes and proceeding to ignore me for the rest of the trip, breathing slowly in and out with a look of concentration so intense I wanted to bundle her up and kiss the hell out of her. What had I done to deserve this wonderful woman?

SAGE

When I'd told Kade that we should go straight to the

hospital, I'd been thinking about the fact he needed to be with his mom and sister. But as we made our way through the hospital to the elevator, heading to the room his mom had directed us to, it occurred to me that I was about to meet his family. The circumstances left a lot to be desired, but I wanted them to like me.

The elevator pinged and we stepped off into a corridor that smelled of illness and disinfectant. Kade didn't speak or look at me as his long legs ate up the distance. I scanned the numbers on the doors we passed. Four-twenty-nine. Four-thirty. Four-thirty-one. We stopped outside four-thirty-two. Kade gripped the door handle and slowly turned it, as though wary of what he might find on the other side.

The door opened into a three-bed ward. The bed nearest us was currently unoccupied but a bag on the chair and a discarded jar of peanuts showed someone had been there recently. An elderly woman slept in the middle. At the far end, two middle-aged women stood at the bedside of a pale younger woman who appeared to be unconscious. I glanced at each of the women in turn. The taller of the two had dark hair liberally salted with gray. Even though she was hunched, I could tell she was taller than average. Her companion was shorter and her hair had been dyed a rich shade of red. I assumed these were Kade's mother and his aunt.

The brunette let out a sob as she spotted Kade and rushed across the room toward us. When she was a couple of feet away, she launched herself into Kade's arms. He caught her and wrapped his arms around her tightly. My insides melted at the display of affection for his mom. She sniffled for a few moments, then let him go and stepped back, wiping her eyes on the backs of her sleeves. The redhead approached more slowly.

"How is she?" Kade asked, gazing over at his sister.

"The doctors say she's doing well," his mom said. "She was hit by shrapnel from relatively close range. Some of the cuts are superficial, but there was a lot of tissue damage to her abdomen and she bled internally."

Kade stiffened. "Prognosis?"

"She may have ongoing issues because of the abdominal injuries but they said it could have been much worse." She pressed her lips together, tears filling her eyes. "There's a good chance she'll be medically discharged." She huffed out a shallow breath. "All I feel is relief because it means my baby will be safe." She met Kade's eyes. "Am I a terrible mom to be grateful for something I know she'll be devastated by?"

He kissed her cheek and gave her another quick hug. "No. It's natural to want her safe, but we need to make sure she feels supported and that we help her process what she's going through. It's going to be a difficult road ahead."

"She'll have us," Cathy said. "We'll make sure she has whatever she needs."

My heart felt heavy. I didn't know Audrey, but I could sense the army was important to her and no matter how supportive her family was, she'd have to work through a lot on her own. Still, it was good she had people who cared for her.

"Who's this?" Kade's mom asked, finally seeming to notice me.

Kade placed a hand on my lower back. "Mom, this is Sage. Sage, my mother, Tina."

"It's nice to meet you," I said, offering her my hand. "I wish it was under better circumstances."

"So do I," she replied, gripping my hand for a little longer than necessary. She eyed me speculatively, and I couldn't help wondering what, if anything, Kade had told her about me.

Kade nodded toward Audrey. "I'd like to see her."

Cathy and Tina stepped aside and he strode to stand by Audrey, his footsteps soft on the vinyl floor. His expression contained a combination of pain and regret. I swallowed, knowing from our previous conversation that he no doubt held himself responsible for what had happened. He believed his sister had only joined the army because of him, and he was carrying the weight of that decision on his shoulders.

I moved closer until I was able to see Audrey's face properly, but I kept a respectful distance, not wanting to intrude on a family moment.

Audrey Campbell had the same thick, dark brown hair as her brother and mother. However, while her brother's features were strong and masculine, Audrey had a thin nose, full lips, and delicate cheekbones. Her skin looked nearly white against the dark mass of her hair and there was a faint flush on her cheeks, as though she was running a fever. I got a warm feeling from her even though she was unconscious, and my heart told me she was a good person. Only her face and neck were visible above the blankets. I felt a pang of sympathy at the sight of a strip of white medical tape covering a stitched gash at the base of her throat.

I glanced up and saw Sean standing in the doorway. He jerked his head to the side.

"I'm going to get drinks," I said to the others, needing to feel useful. "What would you like?"

I took orders, then retreated to the corridor.

"How is she?" Sean asked.

"It sounds like she'll recover, but there might be some lasting damage."

He nodded. "At least they've got her back. She's a tough woman. She'll be all right."

"Hopefully." I glanced around, relieved to see the

corridor was empty. It made me feel safer. In a crowd, it would be much easier for someone to get to me. "I'm bringing them hot drinks. Would you mind helping?"

"Sure."

Together, we found the cafeteria, and between us, we managed to carry the drinks back to the ward. I handed them out while Sean took one of the chairs to the doorway to keep watch. I sat near the wall. Nearby, Kade, Tina, and Cathy talked in low voices. Eventually, Kade wandered over and, with a sigh, dropped onto the chair beside me.

"Is there anything I can do?" I asked, eager to wipe the weary expression from his face.

"No, you've done plenty." He tried to smile, but it was weak. "I'm just battling my conscience."

I reached for his hand. "You're not to blame for her getting hurt. Audrey is her own person. Maybe you gave her the idea of joining the army, but she made her own decision and you can't take responsibility for that."

His lips twisted. "Yeah, but I believe that about as much as you believe that you aren't responsible for the deaths of Jessica and Craig."

I flinched, stung by the rebuke. *Touché.*

"How about we both agree to work on it?" I suggested.

"Yeah," he agreed. "I guess we can do that."

23

KADE

I blinked, my eyes gritty, as Mom and Cathy entered the ward, greeting Sean on the way past. I jerked my head toward Sage and raised my finger to my lips, indicating for them to stay quiet. She'd fallen asleep a couple of hours ago, her head resting on my shoulder. We'd stayed with Audrey overnight while Mom and Cathy returned home to sleep. They looked better than they had when they'd left last night, but Mom still had dark circles under her eyes—probably a product of stress and poor sleep. Cathy was faring better, but perhaps the grande-sized coffee clutched in one of her hands had something to do with that.

"How has she been?" Mom whispered as they drew near.

"She hasn't woken yet."

Audrey was no longer being sedated and the doctor who'd spoken to us last had said it was simply a matter of waiting for her body to be ready to awaken.

"Should we worry?" Cathy asked.

I gave my head a slight shake.

Cathy sunk onto the chair beside the bed and clasped Audrey's hand. Mom sat beside me and fished in her pocket for a container of mints. She offered me one and I took it in case I had bad morning breath.

Mom inclined her head toward Sage. "Are you dating her?"

"No, but I'd like to be."

Her lips tilted up in the closest thing to a smile I'd seen in the past two days. "She seems like a lovely girl. Just right to balance out that brooding intensity you have."

My lips twitched as I suppressed a laugh. "I'll keep that in mind."

Beside me, Sage stirred. I gazed down at her, affection welling in my chest. She brushed her hair off her forehead and looked back at me sleepily. It struck me, all at once, that I wanted to see her sleepy eyes every morning for the rest of my life. It felt right to be here with her. Like puzzle pieces slotting into place.

"Is it morning?" she asked huskily.

"Yeah."

She straightened and blushed, catching sight of Mom. "Hello, Tina. How are you today?"

"Better than yesterday," Mom said. "In fact, why don't you two go and have a proper sleep? You must need it. You, especially, Kade."

I grimaced, wondering if the safe house was still ready for us after our last-minute change of plans yesterday. My phone buzzed and I checked it, discovering a new message from Sean, who seemed to have read my mind.

Sean: *The safe house is ready whenever you are.*

I nodded to Mom. "That's not a bad idea. Will you two be okay here?"

She glanced at Cathy. "We'll be fine. Just let us know when you're on your way back. Depending on how long you sleep for, we might be ready for a meal."

"You got it." I stood and held out a hand to Sage. When

my fingers closed around hers, I couldn't help noticing the difference in our size. She had such a steady personality it could be easy to forget how small she was.

We said goodbye and headed back to the car. I drove, taking us on a circuitous route through the city to shake anyone who might be tailing us. Sean took his car a different route, and when we finally arrived at the safe house, he was already parked nearby.

He got out as we approached, and glanced in each direction. "I'm bone tired," he said once we were within speaking distance. "I've called Grant to watch the apartment door. Vic has been medically cleared so we'll position him outside. Would you like me to get Lyle to join you inside? You'll be sleeping, so it might be a good idea to have another pair of eyes on Sage." He lowered his voice. "Or perhaps you'd rather head home to get some proper rest? You must be even more exhausted than I am."

My jaw tightened. "I'm not leaving Sage." I needed to be able to see her with my own eyes to know she was safe. "Don't worry about calling Lyle." I'd wake up if there was an intruder. I could protect her. After all, we'd be sharing a bed. Nothing could happen without me knowing.

Sean frowned. "Are you sure? You're the one always saying how important it is to be at our best."

I gave him a look that said it wasn't up for debate. "I'm sure."

He shrugged. "Your call. I'll come up with you to wait for Grant."

Feeling slightly unsettled, I let Sean take the lead. Once inside, none of us was keen for conversation. I stripped off my clothes and collapsed onto the bed. When I felt the mattress dip beside me, I slung an arm around Sage and drew her close. I was dreaming within minutes.

I woke cocooned between arms capable of carrying the weight of the world, with a broad, lightly haired chest pressed against my back and the soft sound of Kade's breathing in my ear. I smiled, feeling warm, safe, and content. I'd happily have stayed in that position all day if not for the fact we had to go to the hospital to check on Audrey and to give Cathy and Tina a break. I assumed Audrey hadn't regained consciousness because they'd have called if she had.

Keeping my eyes closed, I allowed myself to enjoy lying in Kade's embrace and envision a future where every day might begin this way. My heart filled to bursting and I kissed one of his arms, unable to contain everything I felt for him. I'd always hoped to find a man I'd want to spend my life with, but I'd never expected it to be someone like him. He was better than I'd dreamed of. Strong, dependable, big-hearted, and undeniably gorgeous.

Now if only we could wrap up this whole issue with Richard Getty and Johnathan Baker so we could focus on our new relationship and on the future we might be able to build together. It was a shame we couldn't afford to devote our time to exploring those new feelings the way they deserved. It wasn't often I wished things were different, but it would be nice not to have to worry about when Getty and Baker might come for me.

The back of my throat prickled with emotion. Kade was such a good man. I couldn't believe he didn't think he was worthy of me. Oh well, I'd just have to remind him otherwise every chance I got.

The phone on the nightstand lit up. I frowned. Had someone sent me a message? I considered grabbing it but worried I might disturb Kade. Slowly—so slowly—I eased my arm out from beneath the blankets and reached for the phone. Thankfully, I was able to get it without needing to move my torso, which would surely have woken him. I paused until I was certain his breaths were still gentle and rhythmic, then I brought the screen to my face. It was an unknown number, which meant it wasn't one of the ones Kade or I had programmed into the burner cell. I opened the message.

Unknown: It's Mick. I've thought of something important, but I can't tell you over the phone. It's too risky. Meet me at Sophie's Coffee House in two hours.

Excitement thrummed through my veins. I'd slipped Mick my number but I hadn't expected him to do anything about it. Perhaps he had the information I needed to get Getty and Baker locked up again so we wouldn't have to worry about them anymore. The idea appealed. But before I could respond, I received a second message.

Unknown: No cops, and don't bring your scary boyfriend.

My excitement faded and my brows drew together. My immediate reaction was to refuse. Without the police or Kade as backup, I'd be putting myself in danger. But then, perhaps it was worth it if it meant I could close this chapter in my life and focus on getting to know Kade better.

I bit my lip and placed the phone back on the night-stand, taking note of the time. If I mentioned Mick's invitation to Kade, he'd tell me not to go, or he'd want to come himself and he might frighten Mick away, then we'd never know what he had to tell us.

I could go without telling him. He'd be upset, but he'd forgive me eventually. My stomach curdled at the thought of deceiving him. I didn't like it, but the longer this dragged on, the more chance there was he might get hurt. Besides, his family needed him more than I did right now, and with

Audrey in the hospital, he might be distracted, his instincts not as sharp. He'd be more likely to mess up. I couldn't stand it if anything happened to take him away from them when I might have been able to prevent it.

I did a quick web search for Sophie's Coffee House. It was a ground floor shop on a road with plenty of pedestrians. If anything went wrong, I should be able to get away, and I had Kade's spare gun, mace, and my crystals for protection. If Mick had suggested I meet him somewhere private, like his apartment, I might have been concerned because there would be plenty of opportunity for someone to incapacitate him and set a trap, but the coffee house would be safer. I could look through the window and if he wasn't there, then I'd take the nearest taxi and disappear, no harm done.

I nibbled my lower lip. I still wasn't comfortable with the idea, but I couldn't think of a better option. Perhaps I'd be able to find out whatever Mick knew, get back here, and have the whole thing wrapped up by lunchtime. It was worth the risk. Protecting Kade and his family was worth everything.

Heart pounding, I sent a reply.

Sage: See you then.

I deleted our messages, placed the phone back on the nightstand, and snuggled against Kade's chest, praying to the universe that I wasn't about to make the worst mistake of my life.

24

Kade woke when I tried to edge out of the bed.

"Where are you going?" he asked, immediately alert. That seemed to be one of the downsides of being with a military veteran. He didn't need much of a waking up period. He could be ready for action in two seconds flat.

I drew in a slow, steady breath, afraid he'd be able to sense my nerves. "Just making breakfast."

"I'll join you." He swung his legs off the bed and strolled around it stark naked. I tracked his movements, unable to look away. He truly was a magnificent man, and he wore the signs of a dangerous life proudly on his body. Scars decorated his back, torso, and arms. I wondered if he'd tell me about them one day.

He stopped, noticing me staring, and cocked a brow. "You get a good look?"

My face flushed. "I like looking at you."

His expression softened and he tilted my chin up and brushed his lips over mine. "Same goes, sweetheart."

My heart jumped wildly and I tried not to melt against

him. I couldn't afford to lose my wits when I was intending to sneak out soon.

"Are raspberry and cacao oats okay?" I asked a little more briskly than necessary.

A flicker of longing crossed his face—no doubt for a staple like bacon and eggs—but he nodded. "Yeah, that's fine."

I dressed and put on a pair of sneakers, hoping he wouldn't notice. I didn't want to have to stop and grab my shoes later. He tugged on a pair of sweatpants but no shirt. In the kitchen, I heated oatmeal in a pot while preparing other ingredients, then poured it into the bowl and layered raspberries, cacao nibs, and seeds on top.

Kade and I ate at the table. I stayed quiet, mentally running through what I'd need to do in order to meet Mick. We no longer had an additional bodyguard inside since Kade had told Sean not to bother sending anyone else, but there was one at the door and another stationed at the building's main entrance.

"Hey."

I glanced up at Kade's sharp tone. "Yeah?"

"You okay?" He looked concerned. "You're hardly eating."

I flashed my teeth in an unconvincing smile and nodded. "Just worn out." I made myself eat a few mouthfuls so I'd at least be fueled for whatever might come, and then tidied away my dishes. When Kade started to do the same, I took his bowl from him. "Let me."

He hesitated, his dark eyes searching mine, but he seemed to find whatever he was looking for. "I'll have a shower and then we can decide what to do next."

"I'll be here." Shame seethed in my gut. I didn't want to lie to him, but I couldn't afford to miss out on the opportunity to make this the mess from my past go away, and Kade needed to focus on his family.

I strained my ears as he left the room. The instant I heard the shower start, I scrawled a quick note and left it on the counter, then I grabbed the gun from my purse and stuffed it into my pants. The mace went into one pocket and my black tourmaline protection stone into the other, along with my phone and a credit card.

I opened the window closest to the adjoining apartment and perched in the frame, wondering whether I was about to make a terrible mistake. I wasn't cut out for behaving like some kind of cat burglar. But then an image of Craig flashed through my mind, quickly followed by the faces of Kade's family members, reminding me I had to keep him safe and keep them all together. I rolled up my metaphorical sleeves, clambered through the window and onto the balcony next door, then leaned over to push the window shut.

I glanced into the old lady's apartment but there was no sign of her. She must be still in bed. I leaned over the edge of the balcony, relieved to see that the apartment below had a similar balcony. I climbed over the railing, sweat beading on my upper lip as I fought not to look down. My arms burned as I lowered myself to the balcony below. Thanks to years of yoga, I was able to land without hurting myself.

I looked around, taking stock. If I recalled what Sean had said correctly, the apartment below ours was empty. Unfortunately, it didn't have a balcony so I couldn't climb over easily. I could try dropping down another couple of stories the same way I'd come to this one. But when I reached ground level, the guard at the entrance would no doubt notice me as I dropped from the sky.

I pursed my lips and glanced at the window of the apartment next door. I needed to act quickly in case someone saw me. Making a decision, I yanked off my sweater and used it to cushion the butt of the gun. I double-checked that none of the metal was exposed, then reached over the balcony and smashed the covered gun into the window of the empty apartment. The glass cracked but didn't shatter. I frowned. They made this look easier in the movies. I tried again. On the third attempt, a starburst of glass crumpled inward. I tucked the gun back into my waistband and covered my hand with the sweater so I could remove the loose glass, then I gingerly took hold of the window frame and pulled myself across.

A hot slice of pain across my palm let me know I'd cut the skin, but I kept going. When I was safely inside, I took a moment to mentally apologize for the damage and promise to replace the window before hurrying to the exit. There was every chance somebody had heard the break-in, so I didn't have long to get away. I unlocked the door and let myself out, then hurtled along the corridor until I reached a door labeled 'Fire Exit'. I raced down the external stairs until I reached the ground.

Pausing to catch my breath, I wondered whether to keep the jacket around my hand or if I'd be better off using it to mask the gun. Hiding the gun was the more pressing matter, so I unwrapped my hand and tied the sweater around my waist. Not much of a fashion statement, but it should hide everything important. I glanced down at the cut on my palm, which was trickling a steady stream of red. Unfortunately there wasn't much I could do about it, so I curled my fingers into a fist to cover the injury and fell into step behind a group of pedestrians.

With my left hand, I used my phone to find directions to Sophie's Coffee House. It was a long walk, but I didn't want to risk getting a taxi. When I passed a restaurant with outdoor tables, I snatched a couple of napkins and balled them in my hand. Someone bumped into me and I jolted in shock. Every loud sound made me flinch, and adrenaline had amped up my senses so much that I felt like I was high on something.

By the time I reached the coffee house, I was longing to sit down. I scanned the collection of small metal tables out front, my curiosity piqued when I saw Mick sitting behind one of them. He was early. But I had no complaints about his choice of seating because it would make for an easier getaway if needed.

"Hey," I said as I approached.

He raised his eyes and I cursed inwardly. His pupils were pinpricks, and based on the sheen of sweat on his forehead, I had to wonder whether he actually had anything useful to tell me or if he'd just gotten high and become paranoid.

"You came." He sounded taken aback.

"I said I would." I drew a chair out with my left hand and was about to sit when something cold and metallic pressed against the small of my back.

"Keep walking," a male voice murmured near my ear. "Don't scream or do anything stupid."

Black spots appeared in my vision and I stumbled.

"No funny business," the man hissed, jabbing what felt like a gun harder into my back. "Walk."

"I'm sorry," Mick mouthed.

He'd sold me out. I couldn't believe it. He'd been my dad's best friend.

How could he?

I tried to open my heart to forgiveness. To understand why he might have done it. For money? Drugs? But all I felt was a bitter betrayal.

As the man guided me away from Mick, my thoughts whirled. What should I do? Based on the way nobody had reacted, I had to assume he'd disguised his weapon. I could reach for my gun, but I'd never be fast enough. I subtly patted my pocket, my stomach dropping as I realized the mace was no longer there. It must have fallen out at some point.

I heard a car door being opened and noticed the sedan parked one car ahead. The guy who'd opened the door turned and dread settled in my stomach as I recognized him. Richard Getty. Which must mean it was Johnathan Baker who had a gun to my back. A firm hand landed on my upper arm and directed me toward the open car door. My opportunity to escape was rapidly dwindling. In a moment of desperation, I reached for the gun tucked beneath my sweater and swung it backward, feeling it crack into something solid.

"Fuck!" Baker's voice was laced with pain and the gun disappeared from my back. I lurched sideways, determined to break free, but Getty lunged at me and we wrestled. Raised voices around us suggested that others were finally noticing what was happening. If I could only hold out for a few more seconds...

Something struck one of my knees and my leg gave out. I was roughly shoved into the back seat of the car and the door slammed in my face. I grabbed the handle but the door wouldn't open. Getty flopped onto the passenger seat and leveled a gun at my head.

"That," he spat, "was very stupid. Now, sit down and shut up or I'll decide we don't need you and put a bullet through your thick skull."

Baker leaped into the driver's seat and we screeched away from the curb. I nodded meekly. There wasn't much else I could do. I just had to hope Kade had seen my note and was already on his way.

"How the hell did this happen?" I demanded, thrusting the note into Grant's hand. "Didn't you see her leave?"

He shrugged helplessly. "No one has come or gone through the door and according to Vic, she didn't leave via the building's main exit either."

I cursed. She must have done a spiderman out the window. I'd be impressed if I weren't so goddamn terrified she'd get herself hurt. "Did he check the ground?"

Grant patted my arm. "She didn't fall. He's cleared the perimeter. It's possible she's still inside the building, but it seems more likely to me that she's already on her way to the coffee house."

"Shit." I dragged my fingers through the scruff on my chin. "How did she slip past us? And why?"

Grant cleared his throat. Based on his expression, I knew he was wondering how come I hadn't noticed Sage making an escape through the window. But damn, even though I'd realized something was off with her, I'd never have guessed what she had planned. Perhaps I was still too tired to be thinking clearly, or just too close to her to see what someone else might have. I bit my tongue. If Lyle had been in the apartment, as Sean had suggested, this never would have happened. I shouldn't have been so damned determined to do everything myself.

"We need to get to that coffee house," I said.

My phone pinged. It was Mom. I didn't read the text. Finding Sage was more urgent than anything else. I pressed my lips together. The fool woman must have known how dangerous it was to go off on her own. Why had she done it?

Grant spoke into his phone. "Vic is bringing the car around front."

"Good." I hurriedly packed my weapons, grabbed a bulletproof vest, and snatched the keys off the counter. I locked the apartment behind us and we ran to the elevator, which seemed to take fucking forever to arrive. When we reached the ground floor, Vic was double-parked outside. We got in and he pulled away before we'd even had time to shut the doors properly.

I sent a quick message to Ronan to let him know we might need support, then donned the bulletproof vest. Thankfully Grant and Vic were already kitted out.

Traffic was bad, and I wanted to yell at the commuters to get a fucking move on, but I managed to keep my shit together. Getting caught up in a road rage incident wouldn't help Sage.

When we finally drew level with the coffee house, Vic stopped, ignoring the honking horns behind him as Grant and I spilled out. I spotted Mick immediately and beelined for him. His eyes widened as I stalked toward him and noticed his pupils were small and that he was fidgeting with a receipt. Fucking hell.

"Where is she?" I demanded, grabbing him by the collar and hoisting him to his feet. All of my instincts were telling me that something was wrong. "What did you do?"

"Excuse me?" a voice said from behind us.

I spun around and glared at a slight man in wire-framed glasses.

"Are you looking for a brunette, about this tall?" He held up a hand to indicate her height.

"Yeah." I stopped glowering. "Have you seen her?"

He waved the phone he had held to his ear. "I'm on with the police. A few minutes ago, two men shoved a woman into their car and drove off with her. It happened so quickly that nobody had time to stop them."

"Was she injured?" I asked, loosening my grip on Mick, who stumbled and fell.

"Nothing serious, as far as I could tell," the guy in glasses said. "But she fought them. She dropped a gun. My friend has it."

I glanced at Grant, who was already making a phone call, presumably to Ronan. "Let me see it." I glared down at Mick. "Don't let this asshole leave. He sold her out."

Glasses waved at an overweight man who was holding a gun awkwardly, as if he'd never touched one before. My stomach sunk. It was Sage's. I hadn't really expected anything else, but I'd hoped.

Sirens screeched and a police car turned onto the block and raced toward us. As it drew alongside, Joanna got out of the passenger seat.

I pointed to Mick. "Take him in for questioning."

She frowned, looking a bit put out at being given orders, but nodded. She turned to Glasses. "Are you the one who reported the abduction?"

He nodded.

"Thank you. Because of your quick actions, we have a better chance of catching up to them."

"Boss," Grant said, touching my arm.

"What?"

"We need to start our own search."

I sighed. "I know. Just let me call Mom and tell her I'll be delayed."

"I'll get Vic to bring the car back around."

"Thanks."

While Joanna continued speaking to Glasses and Grant called Vic, I phoned my mother.

"Hey, honey," she said. "Are you on your way back?"

I winced. "Unfortunately, something has come up at work."

"Something more important than your comatose sister?" Her tone was chilly.

"It's Sage," I admitted. "She's been abducted."

"Oh." She sounded shocked. "I didn't realize she was one of your clients."

I rubbed my throbbing temple. "It's kind of an unofficial thing."

"Whatever that means," she muttered. "Okay, I understand. Let me know when she's safe and don't worry, we'll hold the fort here. Good luck."

I thanked her and hung up. Then I made another call. One I'd really rather not make, but I knew I had to. I'd tried to do everything myself once before and it had bitten me in the ass. It was time to do things differently. Zeke answered just before the call went to voicemail.

"I need your help," I bit out. "Sage has been taken."

25

———

KADE

As I arrived at the King's Security offices, everyone got the hell out of my way. I marched through the warren of cubicles and computers where Zeke's staff were based and let myself into his office. He was sitting behind the desk, a wall of monitors in front of him.

"Why didn't we have eyes on her?" I demanded. "Shouldn't there have been a security camera in the safe house so someone could have raised the alarm as she was trying to leave?"

Zeke arched one pierced eyebrow as he glanced up, clearly not bothered by my belligerent attitude. "Generally, we're trying to keep people *out* of our safe houses, not *inside* them."

I swallowed a sound of frustration. What good was it being part of a billion-dollar company if we didn't take advantage of all of the perks—such as state-of-the-art, real time camera systems?

"I don't understand how a sweet little yoga teacher managed to sneak past trained security personnel with some of the best resourcing in the country," I snapped.

Finally, a flicker of anger crossed Zeke's face. It was the most genuine emotion I'd ever seen out of him. He stood and rounded the desk, then jabbed a finger into my chest.

"Look, Campbell." His tone was low and dangerous. "I know you and I don't often see eye to eye, and a lot of that is on me. I've always enjoyed winding you up. But how about, instead of blaming everyone else for losing your girl, you take a good look in the mirror."

I frowned. What did he mean?

"I spoke to Sean earlier," Zeke continued. "He told me he'd suggested having Lyle inside the apartment but you vetoed the idea. Lyle wouldn't have needed to shower. He'd have had no reason to let Sage out of his sight and she might still be tucked up safely inside that apartment. But you thought you knew better." He grimaced. "You need to be a better team player."

I gaped. Me? A better team player? "That's rich, coming from you."

Zeke rolled his eyes. "You don't approve of my way of doing things. I get it. But that doesn't mean I'm wrong." He backed off a few steps and jerked his head toward the wall of computer monitors. "Come on, I'll show you what we've got."

I rounded his desk, feeling chastised and a little ashamed. Here I was taking out my frustration on him when he was only trying to help. Both Sage and my mom would be disappointed in me. Hell, *I* was disappointed in me.

"Watch this." He hit play on what looked to be poor-quality security camera footage. On the screen, I saw Mick arrive at the coffee house and take a seat. Zeke fast-forwarded through some of the footage, then hit pause. "That's her," he said, pointing to a figure who'd just come into view. He started it playing again. "She says something but before she has time to sit down, Baker comes up behind her."

I watched, a sour taste in my mouth, as a nondescript man guided Sage away from the table, his body language indicating he was holding something to her back. I was tempted to ask why no one had noticed, but playing the blame game wasn't going to help anyone.

Zeke clicked out of the footage and opened another video clip. This one was clearer and from a different angle. It showed Getty opening the door of a sedan. Sage and Baker appeared and I watched, my heart in my mouth, as Sage attacked Baker and then, having bested him, began to struggle with Getty. Even though I knew the outcome, I found myself mentally wishing she'd make a clean escape. But no, she was bundled into the sedan and they took off before anybody could intervene.

"Damn," I growled.

"That's not all." Zeke brought up a map of the city, with several small red dots on it. "Jonah was able to get the license plate and did a city-wide search of traffic cameras. They passed by these," he dragged his finger along the route set out by the red dots, "and were last captured entering this industrial district." He clicked a check box and a smattering of gray dots appeared. "These are all the known traffic cameras in the area. They weren't captured on this one or this one," he showed me the ones he meant, "so it's possible they're still within that district. Perhaps they've found an abandoned warehouse or rented a storage container to use as a base."

I circled the area with my finger. "You think they're somewhere in here?"

He shrugged. "It's my best guess, but Jonah is keeping an eye on the camera information in case the license plate is pinged again."

Some of the tightness around my chest eased. "This is good. Have you told the cops?"

"Already sent it to Jo." He typed something, clicked, and then my phone buzzed. "You have the map now too."

"Thanks." The back of my throat ached. "I appreciate you dropping everything to look into it. I'm, uh, sorry for being a jerk."

Zeke heaved an overly dramatic sigh. "Apology accepted. Just don't do it again."

I clapped him on the back. "Thanks." My tone was gruff. "I'll be in touch when I've got her."

"You'd better." He flashed me a quick smile. Not the fake, too-charming one he usually wore, but something small and sincere that I wasn't sure I'd ever seen from him before. He waved a hand. "Shoo."

I headed to Ronan's office. He was pacing back and forth in front of the windows overlooking the city, talking rapidly to someone on the phone. When he saw me, he held up a finger. A few moments later, he pocketed the phone.

"Joanna is assembling a task force to search the industrial district Zeke tracked them to," he said.

"When are they leaving?" I demanded.

He hesitated, as if unsure whether to tell me.

"King," I warned. "I need to know."

"She estimates they'll be ready to go in an hour. They'll begin at the south end, set up road blocks to the north, west, and east, and search one block at a time."

"But that will take too long," I protested.

He gave me a look. "They have to be methodical and do it by the book. You know that."

I felt cold inside. Technically, he was right, but I couldn't risk anything happening to Sage. Not so soon after finding out about Audrey's condition. I couldn't handle it. Especially not if there was anything I could have done to stop it.

"*They* do," I agreed, meeting his eyes. "But *I* don't."

With a pang of guilt, I realized I was doing the exact thing Zeke had accused me of, but I couldn't help it. I turned on my heel and left.

"Don't do anything stupid!" Ronan called after me.

I shook my head. I wasn't being stupid. I was doing what had to be done. I needed Sage to be safe. I needed *her*, full stop. It was early days, but I was fucking crazy for her and if I found out she'd been hurt, I'd hunt down the bastards responsible and make them pay.

I went straight to the garage, knowing Ronan would try to stop me if I gave him time to react. I chose the most tank-like vehicle in the fleet and got behind the wheel. I didn't stop until I was out of the building, then, I pulled over and called Zeke.

"You're going lone vigilante?" He sounded like he couldn't decide whether he wanted to cuff me over the head or high-five me.

"No," I said. "Not exactly. I'm hoping I'll have you for technical support. If you had to guess where they'd be hiding out within the area you showed me, where would you pick?"

He gave me a couple of addresses and I made a mental note of them.

"Seriously, man," he added. "Be careful."

I sighed. "I will, but if anything happened to Sage, I couldn't handle it. I have to do something."

Zeke was quiet for a moment. At last he said, "I can't say I understand, but I'm glad you're at least keeping me in the loop. I'll get the team working to see if we can narrow down the location. Good luck."

I jabbed the End button and resumed driving. I no longer felt afraid, just steely and determined. Nobody would take Sage from me.

Baker pulled up outside a run-down building that might once have been used as a warehouse. The walls were a patchwork of scruffy white and brown and it had no windows. It looked like the type of place that would be used in a film as a mobster's lair.

"Get out," Getty barked, the gun still aimed steadily at my face. He hadn't wavered since Baker had gotten behind the wheel. Years of prison seemed not to have impacted his ability to handle a gun.

"I can't," I reminded him.

He grunted, got out himself and yanked my door open. "Don't make a fucking sound."

I kept my mouth shut. I didn't have a death wish. I wanted to get out of this situation in one piece so I could apologize to Kade for being so stupid, and hope he forgave me.

A chill ran up my spine as Getty marched me toward the building. I couldn't help thinking about how my silence now echoed what I'd experienced the first time these men had intruded on my life.

The building only seemed to have one door, with a shiny new lock attached to the front that looked out of place. Baker unlocked it and Getty shoved me inside. I tripped but didn't fall. The interior of the warehouse was dim and nearly empty. Trash littered the floor—old pipes and canisters left over from whatever used to be here, food wrappers, and the remnants of a filthy blanket. The walls were riddled with mold and the air smelled of decay. Several columns held the roof in place.

Getty grabbed my shoulder and roughly directed me to

stand beside one of them. "Put your arms around it," he ordered.

I did, keeping my posture stiff and my body away from the timber, not wanting to touch anything in here. It was disgusting. Baker stood on the opposite side of the beam and looped something around my wrists. He pulled it tight and I winced as plastic cut into my skin—perhaps a zip tie.

"Right." Baker sounded pleased. "Now you're not going anywhere."

"What do you want?" I asked, taking care to keep my tone neutral. I tried to look over my shoulder, but with the position I was in, it proved difficult.

"What the fuck do you think we want?" Getty snarled. "Tell us where the money is."

"I don't know."

Baker grabbed my hand and a moment later, white-hot pain blazed through me. I screamed.

"That was for pistol-whipping me." Baker moved into my line of sight. "One finger down, nine to go, unless you decide to do the smart thing."

He'd broken my finger?

Tears streamed down my cheeks and I bit my lip. "I told you, I don't know."

Baker pretended to pout. "Wrong answer." He reached for my hand and I squealed and tried to pull back. He seized my left index finger and dug his nails in. "This one next, I think. What do you reckon, Rich?"

"Good a place to start as any," Getty agreed from somewhere behind me. I felt a cold finger trace down the side of my cheek and shuddered. He leaned close and his breath whispered across my ear as he spoke. "Think really hard. You and your precious mommy knew that lying sack of shit better than anyone. You knew where he'd keep the things that mattered to him."

Precious.

For some reason, that triggered a memory.

During my conversation with Dan, he'd used the same word when he said that I was the most precious thing in my father's world. At the time, I'd felt like I was missing something but hadn't been able to think what. Now, I closed my eyes and imagined Dad's voice as he stood over my bed and told me that everything precious to him was right there.

He'd meant me, of course, but what if that wasn't all he'd meant? What if he'd been trying to give me a clue about where he liked to keep his valuables, in case I ever needed to know?

Surely not.

I shook my head. It was too far-fetched. Besides, someone had already torn apart the mattress. But then, there was more to a bed than the mattress, and Dad had always been crafty.

"Nothing?" Baker asked, tightening his grip on my finger.

"Wait!"

They both stiffened.

Getty grabbed my hair and yanked my head back. "What?"

"The bed," I gasped. "Try my bed at our old house."

"We've already looked there." Disappointment laced his tone.

"But did you check for hidden compartments?" I persisted, not caring that I might be giving them the knowledge they needed to find the money. As far as I was concerned, they could have it. The police would catch up to them anyway. My highest priority was to get myself, and everyone who'd been trying to protect me, out of this unharmed.

"No," Baker said slowly. "We didn't."

"Try it," I urged.

Getty dug his fingertips into my scalp. "What makes you think it's there?"

"Just a feeling." I squeezed my eyes shut. "Something he used to say to me when I was younger."

Getty released me, and I bit my lip so I wouldn't whimper. My hand was throbbing and blood had rushed to my scalp so everything prickled.

"I'll go," Getty said. "Keep her here."

Baker dropped my hand, frowning. "Why don't we both go? It's not like she can get away."

"Because you look like someone smashed you in the face, asshole. It'll draw attention."

A thread of hope worked through me. Perhaps I'd be able to take advantage of this disagreement.

"He's going to cut you out," I said to Baker.

Fire blazed across my cheek as Getty struck me. "Shut your mouth."

The skin above my cheekbone throbbed, and I struggled to draw air into my lungs from the shock of the attack, but I didn't let it deter me.

"If he takes the car and finds the money, what's to stop him from leaving without you?" I pushed.

Baker scowled at Getty. "She's got a point. How do I know you won't run off with the cash like her daddy did?"

Getty growled in frustration. "Because we're partners, John. Have I ever let you down before?"

"No," Baker conceded. "But there's no reason we both can't go. I'll wear a hat and keep my head down."

"You're staying the fuck here."

The two men circled around each other.

"I don't like it," Baker said.

"It'll be fine," Getty tried to assure him. "Why don't you

have fun with our guest while I'm gone? Just don't break her. We might need to save that for later."

A shiver rippled through me.

Baker looked shifty. He clearly wasn't comfortable with the plan. "I don't know, man."

"Fine." Getty shrugged. "Come. I'll start the car. You make sure she isn't going anywhere."

Baker relaxed slightly. "Yeah, okay."

"Good. I'll be back." My stomach churned as Getty's footfalls faded away and the door clicked open. Baker moved closer. I tensed, wondering if I'd have a chance to break free now that I was temporarily alone with a single captor. I had to be ready for anything.

26

KADE

I struck out at the first of the addresses Zeke gave me, but just as I was approaching the second on foot, I spotted a black sedan parked out front, with a man opening the driver's side door. Richard Getty. He looked up and his eyes widened. He glanced from me to the warehouse and back again, then leaped into the car and started the engine. I aimed a shot at the tires as he careened onto the street, but it missed, and a couple of seconds later, he was out of reach.

I froze for a moment, wondering whether to go after him, but he'd definitely been alone in the car, which meant he didn't have Sage, so I turned to the warehouse instead. I half-expected an ambush as I ran toward the warehouse door. It stood open.

"What the fuck are you doing, Rich?" a man's voice asked as I hesitated just outside.

Fear made my breath burn down my throat. What if I was too late? They might have realized Sage couldn't help them and decided it would be easiest to get rid of her. I had no way of knowing she hadn't been in the trunk of the sedan. I wrapped my fingers around the grip of my personal handgun, with one around the trigger, ready to fire. I'd just have to go in and find out. I charged into the cavernous open space, raising my gun to aim at the lone man standing near one of the columns. He dove sideways, behind Sage, using her as a shield.

Her head snapped up and her eyes locked on mine, white with terror. I inventoried her features, relieved to see her face was relatively unblemished, but then I lowered my gaze to her hands and felt sick. One of her fingers was bent at an unnatural angle. Baker glanced from me to the door, and I realized it was the only exit. I blocked it.

"Rich is gone," I told him as calmly as possible. "You're not getting out of here."

"He's d-dead?" he stammered.

My lip curled. "No, he left you here like a goddamned coward."

"Fuck."

"You may as well surrender," I said. "You can't win this."

"That's what you think." He reached around Sage, who was deathly still, and extended something—a knife?—to snip the zip tie around her wrists, then he used one arm to hold her in place and with the other, he put a gun to her temple. "Let me out or I shoot the girl."

My knees felt shaky and I thanked God that I didn't waver.

"You hurt her and I'll kill you," I growled as he circled around, taking her with him.

I edged further into the building, away from the door, giving him enough space that he hopefully wouldn't do anything stupid. He continued advancing, dragging Sage along.

"I can't let you take her out of this warehouse," I said, briefly catching Sage's eyes so she'd know I was talking to her as much as to him. "If you get her through that door, you won't release her."

I knew this because that's what I'd do in his shoes. We were opposite each other, with the door between us. He could push her away and run for it, but I doubted he'd try. He knew I'd shoot him.

He shifted closer. A subtle movement caught my attention. Sage was stealthily reaching into her pocket with her uninjured hand.

What was she doing?

Her hand eased out again, a black stone wand clasped in her grip. I nearly rolled my eyes. It was one of her damn protection crystals.

"Put the gun down and I won't shoot her," Baker ordered.

I hesitated. I didn't want to surrender my weapon, but keeping Sage safe was the only thing that mattered now. If I didn't do as he said, he might act rashly. Slowly, I began to lower the gun to the ground. My gaze caught once more on Sage's fist, which had curled around the long, pointed stone. She widened and narrowed her eyes as though trying to silently communicate with me, but I had no clue what she wanted to get across. She clearly had an idea, but I couldn't tell what. I'd have to trust she knew what she was doing. I had no other choice. Our safety was in her hands now.

She and Baker were nearly in the doorway now, and the tip of my gun touched the floor.

Then, all of a sudden, Sage simultaneously dropped to her knees and rammed the crystal back into Baker's crotch. He howled, curled over, and reflexively squeezed the trigger. Taking advantage of his momentary distraction, I snapped my gun up and shot him in the head. Blood sprayed over Sage, who was still kneeling at his feet. He staggered backward and fell with a dull thud.

I rushed over and kicked his weapon away. The light was already fading from his eyes. Certain he was no longer a threat, I sunk to my knees beside Sage. "Are you okay?"

She raised her eyes, her complexion waxy, and that's when I noticed the blossom of red soaking through the sleeve of her shirt.

Shit. When Baker had let off a shot, he must have hit her.

"Is it your arm?" I asked.

"Yeah." She sounded faint. "Is he...?"

I nodded in answer to her unfinished question. "We need to get your shirt off so I can stop the bleeding."

Her lips curled up tremulously. "If you wanted my shirt off, that's all you had to say."

Despite myself, I chuckled, and relief finally bowled through me. Sage had pulled through. She'd saved both of us. Well, her and the information from Zeke's team.

Zeke.

I pulled a face. He'd been right all along—not that I'd ever tell him as much. I couldn't have done this on my own.

"Fuck, you're amazing." I dropped a light kiss on her lips. "Here." I took hold of the hem of her shirt and slowly worked it up. She hissed and clenched her teeth as she raised her arm, but once it was off I balled the shirt up, glanced at the wound, then pressed the wadded-up shirt to it. "Looks like a graze," I told her. "A deep one, but it shouldn't have done any serious bone or muscle damage."

"A graze?" She sounded like I'd insulted her, and my smile widened. "Feels like more than that."

"You got lucky." I kissed her cheek and helped her ease into a seated position. "You and that damned stone."

"Hey," she protested. "It saved the day."

That time, I did roll my eyes. "I don't think it was the

magic of the crystal that saved you. It was good thinking and a hard object."

"Disbeliever," she teased. But then her face pinched with pain. She brought the hand with a broken finger up to study it and for the first time I noticed a gash across her palm. The blood seemed to have set at some point but she'd opened it again when she'd struck Baker.

"We need an ambulance." I grabbed my phone and called 911 to report the incident, then phoned Ronan and Zeke.

Sage was steadily growing paler as shock set in. She'd been through a lot in a short amount of time. A cut, a broken finger, and now a bullet wound—all while she was flecked with someone else's blood. I sat beside her, wishing I could hug her close but knowing that would likely cause her more pain.

"Why did you do it?" I asked, my voice ragged. "You could have told me Mick had contacted you, and we'd have worked something out."

She reached for my hand with her wounded one and I gently held it carefully to avoid her broken finger. "I love you," she said. "I knew you wouldn't let me go alone, but I thought you needed to focus on your family. I didn't want to get you hurt, and I hoped I might be able to get everything sorted out myself."

I shook my head incredulously. "I love you too." I brought her hand to my mouth and gently kissed the back of it. "So please, for the love of God, don't ever risk yourself like that again. We're a team. That means we talk things through. You told me at the start of all this that relationships are built on trust. I thought I understood, but I didn't. Not fully. Now, I do, and I want that, with you."

Behind us, Baker's phone rang, cutting the moment short.

"That reminds me," Sage said. "Getty is on his way to my old house. He might already be there."

"I'll send reinforcements after him." I could hear sirens approaching fast. "He won't get away." I got to my feet, then squatted and lifted her into my arms. "Let's get you the help you need."

With that, we emerged into the sunlit morning just as an ambulance screeched into view. The cavalry had arrived.

KADE

Once again, I found myself sitting beside a hospital bed while a woman I loved lay pale-faced and asleep. A doctor had cleaned and stitched her wounds and splinted her finger. They'd given her a sedative beforehand and a bunch of painkillers, which I was grateful for because she'd hardly reacted as they worked on her. If she'd been visibly in pain, I might have made a scene.

Unfortunately, the ambulance had taken Sage to a different hospital from the one Audrey was in, so Mom wasn't able to drop by to see how she was and I couldn't check on Audrey, but I'd sent Mom a message to let her know everything was going to be all right and she'd updated me that Audrey was starting to show signs of coming around.

I heard male voices in the corridor and then Willow appeared in the doorway, her eyes red and puffy, tears streaming down her cheeks.

"How is she?" she demanded, rushing to Sage's bedside. "She's unconscious?"

"Just for now," I replied. "It's nothing to worry about. They sedated her so it would be easier to treat her injuries, that's all."

"Oh, good." She flopped onto a chair and all the breath whooshed out of her. "I was so worried."

"So was I."

I turned back to the doorway, where Ronan was standing, and inwardly cringed at his black expression. Zeke had quietly entered and was hovering in the corner, his lips twisted in a strange smile.

"Sorry," I muttered.

"Do you have any idea how dangerous it was for you to go off half-cocked like that?" Ronan asked, rounding on me. "You put yourself at risk, and you put Sage at risk."

"I know." I felt a little shamefaced. "I'm sorry. Having Sage in danger like that made me crazy." While I knew I'd acted rashly, Sage might have been relocated or killed if I'd delayed. I couldn't regret anything that had ended with her being safe.

"Oh." Ronan had clearly not expected that response. "Well, I get it. I wasn't exactly sane after Willow was kidnapped. Still, Joanna is going to tear you to pieces."

I nodded. Whatever telling-off I got from Joanna, I'd sit through it a hundred times to have Sage in one piece.

Zeke clapped my shoulder. "Cheer up. You'll be pleased to hear that Getty has been arrested and there will be a few years added to his sentence."

"It's not enough." He'd been indirectly responsible for eighty percent of the bad shit that had happened in Sage's life. He deserved to rot.

"That's assuming he survives," Zeke added slyly.

I narrowed my eyes. "What do you mean?"

He gave a lazy shrug. "Just that Parrish wasn't happy to be left behind. I'd say Getty has earned himself at least one enemy on the inside."

Something about the way he said it made me suspicious,

but I let it go. As long as Getty was out of Sage's life, I'd try to put him out of my mind as well.

"Did they find the money?" I asked, thinking back to what had started all of this.

"Yes," Ronan said. "The headboard of Sage's childhood bed had been hollowed out and the cash was stored inside. They're going to check whether the serial numbers match what was stolen."

"Huh. I wouldn't have ever thought to look there."

"Me neither," Ronan said.

"Your free spirit is smart," Zeke remarked. "Feisty too." He shook his head, admiration gleaming in his eyes. "I wish I'd seen her nut Baker with the crystal wand."

I grinned. "She's pretty incredible."

On the bed, Sage stirred. Willow turned toward us and shushed, raising a finger to her lips. I nodded and bent over Sage to drop a light kiss on her forehead.

"I love you," I whispered.

27

———

SAGE

I regained consciousness slowly. After a while, I became aware of voices. I tried to latch onto their words but couldn't make sense of them. The tones were familiar and reassuring though—one soft and sweet, the other rough and raspy. My eyelashes fluttered as I willed my eyes to open. At first, all I could see was white, but then details came into focus and I realized I was looking at a ceiling. I turned to the right and gazed into a pair of gorgeous brown eyes. Warmth filled me. I reached for Kade's hand and he slipped it into mine.

"I love you," I murmured, having a vague recollection that I'd already told him so before we arrived at the hospital.

He smiled, and it lit him from within. My heart gave a weak *ka-thunk.* "I love you too, sweetheart."

"So do I," the softer voice added.

I craned my neck further and spotted Willow sitting beside Kade, her expression a mixture of concern and relief.

"How do you feel?" she asked.

I closed my eyes for a moment and tested each of my limbs. Whatever painkillers they had me on must be potent because all I could feel of the wound on my upper arm was a dull burn.

I opened my eyes. "I feel grateful that things worked out all right." I turned back to Kade. "I made a poor decision and I'm sorry I put both of us at risk like that."

His lips pressed together. "We both made mistakes. We're lucky we lived to learn from them."

I sighed. "I should have known there was something suspicious about Mick reaching out to me like that. They must have gotten to him somehow."

"Money," Kade grumbled. "He was in debt and they promised him a share of the cash if they found it. When the police interrogated him, he said he'd tried to tell Getty and Baker that you wouldn't be any help, but they were willing to share the money regardless of whether you led them to it or if they found it another way, so he couldn't see any downside."

"Asshole," Willow hissed.

"He's ill," I said, managing with a bit of distance to find it in my heart to not feel as bitter toward Mick as I had before.

"I'm not forgiving him." Willow's gaze was flinty. "This is one time you can't talk me into doing the forgiveness practice."

I sighed. "Fair enough." To be honest, I wasn't sure I was ready for that myself yet. Understanding was one thing. Forgiveness, another. "So, what else has happened? Did they catch Getty?"

Kade nodded. "He found the money in the hollowed-out headboard of your old bed and was packing it into a duffel bag when the police arrived. They recaptured him and he's been returned to prison."

"Good." I was all for second chances, but Richard Getty didn't deserve a third. "Who ended up with the money?"

"The police. It'll be held as evidence."

I tried to swallow and noticed for the first time that my throat was dry. "Can I get a drink?"

"Sure." Willow passed me a water bottle. I drank from it thirstily until the bottle was nearly empty, then passed it back.

"Baker...?" I left the question hanging.

"He was dead before the ambulance arrived."

I gulped. If I hadn't lashed out at him with my black tourmaline crystal to distract him so Kade could take him down, he might still be alive. For a moment, it felt as though the weight of another death had descended onto my soul, but then I frowned and shook it off.

No. Baker had made his own choices, and the decisions he'd made had led to what happened in that warehouse. His death wasn't my fault. All I'd done was try to protect myself and the man I loved. There was nothing wrong with that.

"I hope you don't blame yourself." Kade reclaimed my hand. "I can see there's a lot going on in your head."

I made a sound of surprise, startled by how well he could read me even though we'd only spent a relatively short time together. Not many people saw through my serene smile, and even fewer called me on it.

"I... don't," I said slowly. "And I'm starting to see that I never should have taken those other deaths onto my conscience. Dad was responsible for what happened to him. Whatever his reasons, he shouldn't have gotten involved with those men, and he especially shouldn't have tried to double-cross them. Mom's death was an accident. Maybe you could say Dad was responsible, but I know he didn't mean for it to happen. Craig's job as a marshal was dangerous. He must have known that, but he chose to do it anyway. He risked himself to save me, and he was the kind of man who I don't think would want me beating myself up over it."

"Of course he wouldn't," Willow said. I sent her a small

smile even though she'd never met Craig and was only saying it out of loyalty.

"What about Jessica?" Kade asked.

I sighed. "That was all Getty and Baker. I'm sorry for what happened to her. She didn't deserve it. I hate how many people have lost their lives over this money."

"Hey." Kade gave me a tender look. "It's over now," he reminded me.

"Thank God for that," Willow exclaimed.

I laughed, but before I had the chance to say anything, Kade's phone rang. He pulled it out of his pocket and accepted the call.

"Hi, Mom." He paused. "She what? Great! I'll be there as soon as I can." He ended the call, his eyes sparkling. "Audrey just woke up."

<hr>

KADE

"I'm coming with you," Sage said, struggling out of the hospital bed.

I stood, wanting to stop her but unsure how to do that without inadvertently hurting her.

"You're not up to going anywhere," I told her.

She narrowed her eyes as if to say, "wanna bet?" "I'm all stitched up and everything is being held in place. I can't see any reason for me to stay here."

"For observation," I suggested.

She huffed. "Go get a doctor. If they tell me to stay then I'll stay, but otherwise, I'm going."

"Fine." I stalked out into the corridor, certain that any doctor worth their salt would agree with me. Unfortunately, the one I brought back didn't.

"You seem perfectly healthy," they said. "Just pick up a

prescription for more painkillers on the way out and check in with your doctor in a couple of weeks for an examination."

Sage arched an eyebrow triumphantly. "Thank you." Her tone was syrupy sweet. "I'll do that."

"Take care," the doctor said, and left again, ignoring my glare burning into the back of her head.

"Here." Willow passed Sage a small backpack. "I brought a change of clothes for you."

To my horror, Sage started to tear up. She sniffled and pulled Willow into a hug. "Thanks, Will." She released her friend and swiped at her eyes. "My emotions are leaking out of my face. I'm just so glad I have you two in my life."

My heart clenched. Despite my frustration with her, I kissed her forehead. "We're the lucky ones."

We left the ward and walked together to the hospital exit, where Willow got into a car Ronan had sent for her. I led Sage around to the parking area. Ronan had left my car there earlier in the day.

"Thanks for coming to save me," Sage said when we were seated in the car.

I reversed out of the parking space and followed the arrows to the junction with the street. "I'll always come for you, sweetheart. You're my wild child." As if there was a universe in which I wouldn't be there for her. "But I think you're forgetting something."

"What's that?"

"You saved me too. If you hadn't stabbed Baker in the balls with that crystal wand, there's every chance he would have shot me, and then he might have shot you too. So really, I didn't save you. You saved both of us."

She beamed. "I like the sound of that."

As I drove, we talked over everything that had happened —and by "we," I meant mostly her. But I listened to her chatter and felt a sense of rightness that went deep to my core. We belonged together and I didn't intend to screw it up for a second time.

It took a while for us to find a parking spot, and then I had to slow my stride through the hospital corridors so Sage could keep up. When I finally cast eyes on Audrey, still lying in the bed with a washed-out complexion and tired blue eyes, my heart lifted.

"Why are you looking at me like a sentimental idiot?" she demanded, her voice much weaker than it usually was. "Get over here and help me escape from these hovering mama bears."

I grinned. "That's the sister I know and love."

I joined Mom and Cathy, who were standing next to the bed, and reached down to ruffle Audrey's hair. "Good to see you've joined the land of the living. You had us worried."

She rolled her eyes. "Not sure what all the fuss is about. It's just a few cuts. I'll be back in action before you know it."

I met Mom's eyes and she grimaced. I returned the expression. I couldn't tell whether Audrey was in denial about the extent of her injuries or just on some good drugs, but things weren't going to be nearly as straightforward as she seemed to think. I wasn't going to be the one to burst her bubble though. Not when she'd just woken up.

Audrey looked at Sage and frowned. "Do I know you?"

"No," Sage replied.

"Thank God. I was afraid I might have lost my memory." Audrey grinned, but seemed disappointed when no one laughed. She glanced from Sage to me and her eyes narrowed. "Don't tell me you're dating my brother?"

Sage caught my eyes, a question in hers, and I nodded. "Yes," she confirmed. "We haven't been together for long though."

Audrey scanned her from head to toe, lingering on the

bandaged hand and splinted finger. "What happened to you?"

"It's a long story."

Audrey smirked. "It's not like I'm going anywhere."

So we sat down and talked. Audrey was fascinated by Sage's life. Mom was too, blinking back tears as Sage explained everything she'd been through. I got the impression she wanted to hug her but wasn't sure whether the gesture would be welcome.

Surprising me, Sage seemed equally interested by Audrey's experience in the military. Perhaps I should have expected it. No matter how gentle and loving Sage was most of the time, she had a core of steel. She and Audrey had that in common.

When Audrey grew weary, we excused ourselves and headed for the King's Security office. I owed Ronan and Zeke a proper apology for going rogue. We stopped at a liquor store on the way and I bought them each a bottle of whiskey. On the way into the building, Sage spotted Willow and Fiona so she joined them while I continued to Ronan's office. He was sitting behind his wooden desk, with Zeke on a chair opposite. Ronan gestured for me to sit. I handed them each a bottle first.

"Thanks," Ronan said, studying the label appreciatively.

"I saw you coming and wanted to make sure you didn't forget to drop my bottle off," Zeke remarked as I passed him his. "I'm not always on your Christmas card list."

"Well, you are now." I tucked my hands into my pockets. "I owe you. There's no way I'd have found her so quickly without you working your magic."

He gave a slight bow. "I do my best."

"So, what next?" Ronan asked. "Will you be back in the office tomorrow?"

I pursed my lips, wondering how to mention the

thoughts I'd been having while I was sitting next to a sleeping Sage earlier. "I might take a few days off."

Ronan nodded. "I expected as much. To be with Sage?"

"Yeah." I gestured to the bottle. "You want to pour us one?"

He raised a brow but drew three small glasses out from a desk drawer and filled each. I took one and tossed it back.

"That isn't how you drink good whiskey," Zeke chided.

I pretended not to hear him. "I'm thinking of asking Sage to move in with me while she recovers."

Zeke's eyes widened. "That's a big step."

I shrugged. "I love her, so it doesn't feel like it. Besides, she can't possibly want to go back to her house after what happened there."

He winced. "I guess not. The poor thing has had bad luck in living situations, hasn't she?"

"You know, if it's just the house that's bothering you, she can stay with us," Ronan said, watching me intently.

One side of my mouth hitched up. "It's not just that. I want her with me."

"Then do it," he said. "But don't make the mistake of asking in a way that sounds like it's just a convenient arrangement." He shuddered. "Trust me, that doesn't go well."

I laughed and raised my empty glass to him. "I'll learn from your mistakes. Thanks, man."

Zeke and Ronan raised their glasses. Then they each sipped their whiskey and I just sat back and smiled. Things were pretty damn good.

28

SAGE

"Here, I got something for you." Fiona pressed a small, gift-wrapped object into my hand.

I looked up at her, surprised. "You didn't have to do that."

"I know." She smiled. "I wanted to. Go on, open it."

I carefully peeled back the layers of paper, exposing a polished black stone. I raised my eyes to her questioningly.

"It's black tourmaline," she said. "To replace the one the police took as evidence. I thought since it did such a good job, you might want to have one to carry with you again. Unfortunately, I wasn't able to find a wand-shaped crystal, so I had to settle for that."

I ran my thumb over the surface of the black heart that sat heavy on my palm. "It's perfect. Thank you."

"What's that?"

I jolted at the sound of Kade's voice and looked up to see him approaching. "A gift from Fiona." I showed it to him. "Isn't that thoughtful of her?"

"It is." He kissed my cheek. "I've finished what I came

here to do. Would you like to come back to my place for the night?"

"Yes, please." Despite the many days we'd spent together, I had yet to see his home.

"Great." He planted his hand on the small of my back. "Are you ready now, or do you need a bit more time to catch up?"

"Now is good." I gave Willow a quick hug, then pulled Fiona into one too. "Thank you both. I'll see you again soon."

"Rest up," Willow ordered.

"I will."

Kade and I left the others and returned to his car. The journey to his home, a charming villa in a semi-suburban area, took a while, but seeing where he lived, I could understand why he bothered to make the commute. The house had a well-kept front garden and a welcoming vibe that made me smile even though we hadn't gotten inside yet. We walked up a cobbled path to the covered porch, where I could imagine us sitting on a comfortable pair of chairs on a long summer evening. He unlocked the door and held it open for me to enter first.

The interior was bright and airy, and my immediate thought was that this was a friendly house. I slipped my shoes off and padded over polished wooden floors through a small foyer, and into the living area. The living room, kitchen, and dining area were open plan, with double glass doors opening onto a backyard large enough for children to kick a ball around. The kitchen was tidy but well-used, and the furniture was nice without being ostentatious.

It felt like a home. Somewhere to raise a family. I loved it.

"This is so wonderful," I said, gazing around and noticing a few family photographs on one of the walls.

"I was hoping you'd think so." Kade gently took my hands in his, his tone even more serious than usual. "I want you to move in with me—at least while you heal."

"You do?" Some people might have been shocked by the statement, but before I could even think it through, joy was buzzing within me, and my intuition said that was everything I needed to know.

"Yeah." He released my hands and brushed the hair off my forehead, his fingers continuing to trace a path down the side of my cheek. "I love you, and I want you close. I'd like to hold you every night, and for you to fill our home with color. Will you give it a chance?"

I rested my head against his chest and breathed in his clean masculine scent. "I would love that."

"Good." Tension eased from him. I hadn't even realized how nervous he'd been. "Let me show you the rest of the house."

He led me down a hall, off which came two bedrooms and a large exercise room with plenty of space for me to set up my yoga gear. A Kade-sized bathtub took pride of place in the bathroom, and more photos of Tina, Audrey, and a man I assumed must be Kade's father were displayed on the walls.

"Where is your dad these days?" I asked.

He paused beside a photograph of a teenage Kade with his father's arm around him and, for a moment, I felt like I could see into his soul. "He died in a car crash."

"I'm sorry." I wound my uninjured arm around his waist and nestled closer.

"It was a long time ago."

"Doesn't mean you don't miss him."

"True." He stared at the photograph for a few more seconds, then turned away and guided me back to the living room. "Why don't you make yourself comfortable on the sofa while I cook dinner?"

"I can help," I said.

He kissed me gently. "Let me look after you, okay?"

Something softened inside me. "Okay."

As I settled on the sofa and watched him prepare dinner, a wave of déjà vu hit me. I felt like I'd sat in this same place and done the same thing a dozen times before. I smiled to myself and silently thanked the universe for bringing me to exactly where I was supposed to be.

<hr>

KADE

After dinner, we retreated to my bedroom and lay naked in each other's arms. There was nothing sexual about it, considering the day we'd had, but it was nice to be close to Sage. To feel her skin against me and know she was safe and well. I rested my hand over her heart and imagined I could feel the steady beat, reminding me I hadn't lost her. I kissed her cheek and carefully tucked her against the side of my body.

"So, want to go to dinner tomorrow night?" I asked.

She tilted her face toward me, her expression curious. "I'd love to."

"Good, because I just realized we've never been on an actual date. Almost all the time we've spent together has been under stressful circumstances, and I can't wait to get to know what you're like when people aren't trying to kidnap you."

She laughed. "I'm much the same. Maybe a little less stabby."

"Only maybe?"

She snuggled closer. "I guess you'll have to keep me around to find out."

My heart warmed. "I'll keep you for as long as you'll have me."

We drifted into silence, and before I knew it, I had my arms full of sleeping woman. I could honestly say I'd never been more content in my life.

29

———

SAGE - THREE WEEKS LATER

Kade and I stood in the living room of my parent's house. Both the front and back doors were open, allowing a breeze to flow through. The place was empty. Over the past week, after the police had once again cleared out, Willow, Kade, and I had removed everything that was here. I'd struggled at first. It had felt like I was saying goodbye to the person I used to be and to the life I'd had with my parents, but it needed to be done. We'd donated what we could and gotten rid of the rest. Now, all that was left was for me to release the last of my emotional ties so the demolition team could start.

"Are you sure you want to do it now?" Kade asked. "There's no rush."

I looked around, and for once, my gaze wasn't drawn to the red smudge on the tiles or the hole in the carpet. Instead, I recalled the good times we'd had here. Closing my eyes, I allowed myself to remember what it felt like to be wrapped in one of Mom's hugs, and how she'd always smelled faintly of lemon. I pictured Dad's smile as he got home and the way he used to spin Mom around before

228

kissing her in greeting. I imagined us happy because we'd been that way once.

"Now is good." I struck a match and used it to set a sprig of white sage alight. We watched as it burned, and just before it reached my fingers, I blew it out and placed the embers on an abalone shell. "Pass me the spray."

Kade handed me a small bottle of homemade Himalayan salt spray and I took it in my left hand, then I circled the interior of the room, murmuring a blessing under my breath as I spread the sage smoke and sprayed cleansing salt into the air. I worked through the house room by room, finishing at the front door.

"Goodbye, and go well," I whispered, a tear trailing down my cheek. I turned to Kade. "It's done."

He embraced me and kissed my forehead. "Do you want to watch?"

"No, I don't need to." I'd said my farewell. There was nothing here for me anymore. At least, there wouldn't be until the construction crew had demolished the house and cleared the grounds. I'd build a new wellness center in its place. It was Kade who'd made the suggestion. It would give me the freedom and independence to do my own thing, and it felt like the perfect way to honor my parents' memory while creating something positive for the future.

I took his hand. "Let's go."

He gestured to the digger driver that they could begin, and as we headed to his car, I heard a crunch behind us but I didn't look back. From now on, I was strictly looking forward.

KADE

Tears prickled in my eyes and my heart was full to

bursting as I took Sage back to our place. I was so proud of her. I knew how hard it must have been to let go of that last connection to her past, but she'd done it and she was going to kick ass with her new wellness center.

Cars lined the street outside our house and I pulled up the drive, which people had thoughtfully left clear. The front door was open and several guests turned toward us as we entered.

Willow was waiting near the entrance and she hurried over and kissed Sage's cheek. "How are you?"

Sage gave the question some thought. I loved how she did that and didn't simply throw out the easy answer the way other people might. "I'm good," she said. "It felt right."

"I'm so glad to hear that." Willow passed her a wrapped gift. "For your center."

Sage opened the gift and smiled widely. "It's perfect." She held up a carving of a woman doing yoga, made out of some kind of clear stone. "Thank you."

"You're welcome."

"The grill is fired up!" Zeke called, sticking his head in through the doors opposite. He caught sight of us and grinned. "Hey, how'd it go? You didn't happen to take a video of the demolition, did you?"

"Don't be insensitive," a woman snapped. Fiona. I rolled my eyes. Those two just couldn't leave each other alone.

"Sorry." Zeke held his hands up defensively and vanished back out the door.

Sage and I moved through the room, greeting friends and family. We'd invited the people we most cared about to be here to commemorate the occasion. My business partners, my family, a few of Sage's friends from yoga, and a handful of King's Security employees. I nodded to Sean, who was leaning against a wall with a beer in his hand, talking to Vic.

"Do you want a drink?" I asked Sage.

"I'll make myself a fruit tea," she replied. "Want me to get you a beer while I'm at it?"

"That'd be great."

She headed to the kitchen and I wandered over to join Ronan and Joanna, who were speaking intently. They broke off as I approached.

"How is she?" Ronan asked, low enough not to be overheard.

"Amazing." I didn't care if I looked and sounded like a sap. "She's so strong. Fucking incredible."

"Glad to hear it." He raised his drink to me in acknowledgment. "Want to weigh in on something for us?"

I glanced between them, noticing the determined set of Joanna's chin and the gleam in Ronan's eyes. "Only if it's not going to get me in trouble."

Joanna heaved a sigh. "It won't. At least, not from me."

I widened my eyes. That sounded like a challenge.

Ronan didn't look bothered. "Do you believe in love at first sight?"

"Um..." The question took me aback. "I don't know. Why?"

"Because Joanna thinks it's possible but I don't," he explained.

"Hmph." Joanna pursed her lips. "Not *love* at first sight, exactly," she said. "But I think it's possible to feel an instant connection. To see someone and know they're going to be important in your life."

I studied her with interest. I'd never thought of Joanna as romantic.

She flushed beneath my scrutiny. "What? Being a cop doesn't mean I have to be cynical about everything."

"I guess not." I cocked my head while I considered the possibility. "Love at first sight, no," I said, and Ronan smiled smugly. "But," I added, "I definitely think an instant attraction or connection can happen. That electric zing."

Joanna arched an eyebrow at Ronan as if to say "See?"

Ronan shrugged. "I guess we'll never know for sure unless we witness it." He glanced toward the kitchen. "Audrey is looking much better."

I followed his gaze and saw my sister chatting with Sage, each of them smiling. I felt a glow inside and wondered if it was visible on my face. I couldn't believe how lucky I'd gotten. I'd found love with a wonderful woman whom Mom and Audrey loved too, my baby sister was healing well, and Sage's presence was evident in every room of my house. She'd put her own touch on the place, with crystals, incense burners, and something called a salt lamp. I'd never have chosen the decor for myself but I loved it because it reminded me of her.

Ronan cleared his throat.

"Oh." I realized I hadn't replied. "Yeah, she's doing well. I think she has more pain from the scarring than she lets on, but the physiotherapist she's working with is great and she's made a lot of progress."

"She's tough," Joanna said.

I winked at her. "Takes one to know one."

She rolled her eyes.

"If she decides to leave the army, you know we'll have a place for her," Ronan said.

I nodded. "I know, but I want her to make that choice on her own. We can't rush her."

Sage looked over and locked eyes with me. I walked toward her, meeting her halfway across the room. Before she could hand me the beer, I kissed her soundly on the mouth.

"Love you," I murmured against her lips.

"Always."

EPILOGUE

I waved the last participant out of the studio and released a huge sigh of relief. The first yoga class at my new wellness retreat, Sage's Soul Care, had been fully booked a week in advance and everything had gone smoothly. The women—and handful of men—who'd shown up had been as enthusiastic and excited as I was. Many had done my online classes or attended sessions I'd led at other gyms, and it had been lovely to see so many friendly faces. I'd kept the yoga itself gentle and nurturing since there were some beginners, and a few people had signed up for a six-week fundamentals of yoga course once the class ended.

I smiled to myself as I tidied the room and switched off the sound system. I'd spent months working toward opening day and it was incredible to see how everything had come together. There had been much more to organize than I ever could have imagined, but I'd loved every second and the center was now exactly as I'd envisioned it. Technically, the first full day of business would be tomorrow. We had a schedule of meditation, yoga, breathing exercises, and crystal healing classes ready to go, but I'd wanted a trial run tonight to make sure there wasn't anything I'd forgotten.

"Hey, beautiful."

I bounced over to the mountain of a man in the doorway and threw my arms around him. "Kade!"

He chuckled and kissed the top of my head as he hugged me back. "No problems?"

I rested my cheek on his chest. "It was absolutely perfect."

"Tomorrow will be too," he assured me. "They adore you. Besides, you wouldn't accept anything less than success."

I breathed in his scent. There was little I loved more than being held by Kade.

"Thanks for coming by." It wasn't exactly on his way home.

He waved at something behind himself. "I brought takeout. Don't worry, I got it from that organic Thai place."

"Perfect." I stretched onto my toes and kissed him. "I'm exhausted. That sounds like exactly what I need."

I threaded my fingers through his and tried to lead him from the room, but he refused to budge. He disentangled his hand from mine. I frowned, a sense of unease coming over me.

But then he sunk to one knee and withdrew a small box from his pocket. He popped it open and I gasped. Nestled on a bed of black velvet was the most breathtaking ring I'd ever seen. A cluster of delicate rose quartz stones encircled a round, multifaceted diamond set in a delicate gold band. Not only was it stunning, but rose quartz symbolized unconditional love, and the fact he'd cared enough to find that out brought tears to my eyes.

"I love you," Kade said. "You've brought sunshine and

joy into my life and every day is better with you in it. Will you be my wife?"

"I'd be honored." I drew him to his feet, cupped his gorgeous face between my palms, and kissed him with all the love in my heart.

He grinned down at me. "Let's see if I guessed your size right."

I reached for the ring, but he stopped me.

"Let me." He took the ring between his finger and thumb and slid it onto the fourth finger of my left hand. It was a perfect fit.

Just like we were.

THE END

EXCERPT FROM THE SPY

FIONA

"Fiona, can you come out to reception, please? The police are here to see you."

I frowned and glanced up from my computer. Stephanie, who worked at the front desk, was hovering in front of me, her face scrunched with apprehension—whether from interrupting me or because of the police's presence, I wasn't sure.

"Is it Detective Lee?"

My boss, Ronan King, the chief executive of King's Security, often liaised with the Chicago police via Detective Joanna Lee.

"No, it's not Joanna. I would have just let her through. It's a man and a woman I haven't met before." Stephanie grimaced. "I asked why they want to see you, but they said it's confidential. Sorry I can't be more helpful."

"It's not your fault." I stood and smoothed the front of my pencil skirt. "I suppose I'd better see what they're here for."

Stephanie's face softened with relief. "Thanks, Fi."

I sent her a reassuring smile. Dealing with the police could be intimidating. I didn't have the best history with them, so it had been difficult for me when I started as Ronan's assistant. Eventually, I'd gotten used to it, and Joanna was always good to deal with. Polite, professional, and only pushy when she felt it was warranted. Other cops still made me nervous.

We strode down the corridor together. I held the door open for her and then followed her into the spacious reception area. High-end artwork hung on the walls and I took a moment to appreciate my favorite—an abstract painting of the ocean in shades of blue, purple, and green—before focusing on the police seated on the designer sofa. Even without uniforms, it was obvious who they were. There was just something about the way a cop dressed and carried themselves that gave them away. Stephanie returned to her seat behind the desk while I made my way to them.

"Hello." I greeted them with a smile. "What can I do for you?"

They stood, and the woman brushed lint off her dark slacks.

"Fiona Ryan?" she asked.

"Yes." I nodded, the back of my neck prickling. For some reason, I had a bad feeling about this. Perhaps it was the way she appraised me as if determining whether I was a flight risk.

"I'm Detective Gloria Harrison and this is my partner, Detective Mark Goodwin. We'd like you to come down to the station so we can ask you some questions."

Internal alarms blared in my head. That wasn't the usual protocol for dealings between King's Security and the Metro P.D.

I forced my expression to remain neutral. "Can I ask what this is about?"

"We'd like to discuss an incident that occurred last night." She glanced around. "We'd prefer not to get into detail until we're somewhere more private."

"I can find a meeting room for us to use," I suggested. My instincts were warning me that going with them wouldn't be wise.

The male cop, Goodwin, put his hand on his hip. "With all due respect, Miss Ryan, we'd prefer to talk to you at the station."

My mouth went dry. Something was definitely off about this. "Is this regarding a King's Security matter? If so, you'd be better off speaking to one of the directors."

Harrison's lips firmed. "It's not."

That's what I'd been afraid of.

I drew in a slow, shaky breath. It seemed my past might be coming back to bite me in the ass. Again. "Can you call Detective Lee? I'd like to speak to her before I go anywhere."

Joanna was sensible. She knew me. Surely, she'd be able to help. But Harrison shook her head.

"Detective Lee is homicide," she said. "She's not in our unit, and she isn't relevant to this discussion."

My heart sped up. It felt as if it was pounding against the inside of my rib cage. A sense of déjà vu swept over me. Once again, the police had come for me, and once again, I was in the dark as to why. Last time, I'd lost my job, my reputation, my boyfriend, and all of my savings. I'd had to start over. Would this time be the same?

No. It couldn't. I had resources available to help me. I wouldn't let history repeat itself.

"I'll come with you. Just let me notify my boss that I'm leaving the office."

Harrison nodded her assent. I went to the reception desk, her sharp eyes following me. I wouldn't go and speak to Ronan in person because I feared they'd insist on accompanying me, and that would create a stir in the office. At least out here there were fewer people to witness my humiliation. I leaned over the desk and spoke softly.

"Stephanie, can you please get Mr. King on the phone?"

She nodded, her eyes wide. "Of course." She dialed the extension for Ronan's office and waited for a moment. "Mr. King? I have Fiona on the line for you." Another pause. I could imagine Ronan would be confused. After all, I was usually the one patching calls through to him, not asking to be put through. "Yes, sir." She handed me the phone.

"Hi," I said, glancing back at the cops and lowering my voice. "I hate to ask, but would you be able to do me a favor?"

"What favor is that?" He sounded bemused.

"Can you please call my attorney and ask her to get to the Metro Police Station as quickly as possible?" I carried on without giving him a chance to respond. "Her name is Ariadne Rodgers. She works at MacBeth and Travers."

"Of course." I heard papers shuffling and hoped he was recording her details. "What's going on?"

"I'm not sure yet." I hesitated, then added, "It could be about those paintings. I don't want to take any risks."

"Would you like me to come and speak to them?" His tone was brusque. "I'm sure we can clear this up."

"Just get Ariadne down to the police station ASAP." It was nice to know Ronan had my back, but I didn't want to cause a scene. Although I was fully prepared to do so later if things went downhill.

"I will. And Fiona, if they make any accusations or ask questions you're unsure how to answer, stay quiet. Silence is always best."

"Thanks, Ronan." I'd learned that lesson myself as well —the hard way. When you don't understand what's going on, it's easy to say things that can be used against you later, or to lose your temper and do or say something you regret. "Hopefully I'll be back soon."

"Be careful," he cautioned, and the phone disconnected. I passed it back to Stephanie and turned to face Detectives Harrison and Goodwin.

"Okay," I said, holding my head high. "Let me get my purse, and then we can go."

Thankfully, they didn't make a production of removing me from the building. After I ducked back to my desk for my purse, we left calmly. I got into the back of their car. They didn't speak during the drive—not to each other or to me—and when we arrived, I was ushered into an interview room.

"Do you mind if I record this conversation?" Detective Harrison asked, placing a voice recorder on the center of the table between us.

I cocked my head. "Do you need to read me my rights first?"

"You're not under arrest. I'd just like to be able to focus on our conversation now and take notes later."

"Okay," I allowed. I didn't intend on saying anything to incriminate myself, so surely it wouldn't hurt.

Harrison switched the device on, then leaned back in her chair and glanced at Goodwin, who rested his forearms on the table and watched me steadily.

"Where is the Monet?" he asked.

ALSO BY A. RIVERS

King's Security

The King

The Veteran

The Spy

Crown MMA Romance

Fighter's Heart

Fighter's Best Friend

Fighter's Secret

Fighter's Second Chance

Crown MMA Romance: The Outsiders

Fighter's Frenemy

Fighter's Fake Out

Fighter's Mercy

Fighter's Forever

ACKNOWLEDGMENTS

Writing *The Veteran* was an absolute joy compared to battling through the first draft of *The King*. Kade and Sage seemed to come to life as my fingers flew over the keys. I absolutely adored them and their story. I did have a few concerns about what the government might think if they were to check my Google search history while I was writing though. There are so many things you don't know you need to know for a book featuring characters with such different life experiences from your own.

Thank you to Serena and Kate for your invaluable feedback and support in editing and proofreading. Thank you to Dinah for helping with the final polish. A massive thank you to Maria for the gorgeous cover, and to everyone on my ARC team who reads and reviews to help make each launch a success. You are amazing.

ABOUT THE AUTHOR

A. Rivers writes romance with strong heroes and heroines who kick butt and take names. She loves MMA fighters, private investigators, military men, bodyguards, and the protective guy next door who isn't afraid to fight the odds for love. She also writes small town romance as Alexa Rivers.

www.ingramcontent.com/pod-product-compliance
Lightning Source LLC
Chambersburg PA
CBHW020909160726
47993CB00005B/1881